HONEY MOON

SHIVER

by
Joyce Magnin

Illustrations by Christina Weidman

Created by Mark Andrew Poe

rabbit publishers

Shiver (Honey Moon)
By Joyce Magnin
Created by Mark Andrew Poe

Rabbit Publishers
1624 W. Northwest Highway
Arlington Heights, IL 60004

Illustrations by Christina Weidman
Cover design by Megan Black
Interior Design by Lewis Design & Marketing

ISBN: 978-1-943785-80-3

10 9 8 7 6 5 4 3 2 1

1. Fiction - Action and Adventure 2. Children's Fiction
First Color Edition
Printed in U.S.A.

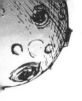

Pay attention to the glimmers.

— Shiver

Table of Contents

PREFACE

Halloween visited the little town of Sleepy Hollow and never left. Many moons ago, a sly and evil mayor found the powers of darkness helpful in building Sleepy Hollow into "Spooky Town," one of the country's most celebrated attractions. Now, years later, the indomitable Honey Moon understands she must live in the town but she doesn't have to like it, and she is doing everything she can to make sure that goodness and light are more important than evil and darkness.

Welcome to the world of Honey Moon. Halloween may have found a home in Sleepy Hollow, but Honey and her friends are going to make sure it doesn't catch them in its Spooky Town web.

FAMILY

Honey Moon

Honey is ten years old. She is in the fifth grade at Sleepy Hollow Elementary School. She loves to read, and she loves to spend time with her friends. Honey is sassy and spirited and doesn't have any trouble speaking her mind—even if it gets her grounded once in a while. Honey has a strong sensor when it comes to knowing right from wrong and good from evil and, like she says, when it comes to doing the right thing— Honey goes where she is needed.

Harry Moon

Harry is Honey's older brother. He is thirteen years old and in the eighth grade at Sleepy Hollow Middle School. Harry is a magician. And not just a kid magician who does kid tricks, nope, Harry has the true gift of magic.

Harvest Moon

Harvest is the baby of the Moon family. He is two years old. Sometimes Honey has to watch him, but she mostly doesn't mind.

Mary Moon

Mary Moon is the mom. She is fair and straightforward with her kids. She loves them dearly, and they know it. Mary works full time as a nurse, so she often relies on her family for help around the house.

John Moon

John is the dad. He's a bit of a nerd. He works as an IT professional, and sometimes he thinks he would love it if his children followed in his footsteps. But he respects that Harry, Honey, and possibly Harvest will need to go their own way. John owns a classic sports car he calls Emma.

Half Moon

Half Moon is the family dog. He is big and clumsy and has floppy ears. Half is pretty much your basic dog.

FRIENDS

Becky Young

Becky is Honey's best friend. They've known each other since pre-school. Becky is quiet and smart. She is an artist. She is loyal to Honey and usually lets Honey take the lead, but occasionally, Becky makes her thoughts known. And she has really great ideas.

IV

Claire Sinclair

Claire is also Honey's friend. She's a bit bossy, like Honey, so they sometimes clash. Claire is an athlete. She enjoys all sports but especially soccer, softball, and basketball. Sometimes kids poke fun at her rhyming name. But she doesn't mind—not one bit.

Isabela Bonito Stevens

Isabela is Honey's newest friend. Isabela volunteers at the Sleepy Hollow Animal Shelter. Animals are her thing, and she has never met a fur baby she didn't love. Honey is showing Isabela the ropes of living in Spooky Town.

FOES

Clarice Maxine Kligore

Clarice is Honey's arch nemesis. For some reason Clarice doesn't like Honey and tries to bully her. But Honey has no trouble standing up to her. The reason Clarice likes to hassle Honey probably has something to do with the fact that Honey knows the truth abut the Kligores. They are evil.

Maximus Kligore

The Honorable (or not-so-honorable depending on your viewpoint) Maximus Kligore is the mayor of Sleepy Hollow. He is the one who plunged Sleepy Hollow into a state of eternal Halloween. He said it was just a publicity stunt to raise town revenues and increase jobs. But Honey knows differently. She knows there is more to Kligore's plans—something so much more sinister.

It is with deep regret that I write this. It has become obvious that our best efforts were no match for the Quiet Ones. They have descended upon our sweet town of Sleepy Hollow, unleashing a sense of fear on young and old. My friends, Samson Dupree and Shiver, and I have used all the weapons in our arsenal, but we could not hold off Halloween. It is coming.

The battle for Sleepy Hollow's soul, we now know, will require the Deep Magic.

In the end, I did uncover their plan to raise up one horrible man who will do their bidding. He will take over and control the town, casting his most evil spell of all to trap the town and its people forever in Halloween. Our beautiful Sleepy Hollow has begun a long and slow decay into nastiness and greed.

By the time anyone reads this journal, I will be long gone. The Quiet Ones' evil deed will have been done. I can only hope that Shiver and Samson are correct when they say two heroes will emerge in Sleepy Hollow who will defeat the wicked Kligore and his denizens of evil. Two heroes, they say, who will share my DNA.
I pray they come soon.

And so, I leave these journals to my friend Shiver in the hopes she can use them to help these two heroes in their quest.

May the Great Magician guide and keep these heroes—whoever they are.

Astronomer Moon

May 1846
London, England

Sleepy Hollow, Massachusetts

In the still, wee hours before the rising sun, while the mist lay thick over the fields, a visitor named Shiver came to Sleepy Hollow with a shop full of treats, a bag full of tricks, and a message for Honey Moon.

THE HIDING PLACE

"**A**BRACADABRA!"

Honey Moon shook her head. She had been listening to her older brother, Harry, practice his magic act all morning when all she wanted to do was spend a quiet Saturday with her friends.

"One more abracadabra and I'm gonna

scream."

"Oh, it's not so bad," Becky Young, Honey's best friend, said. "He needs to practice."

"Yeah but why does he have to do it now?"

Becky shrugged. "What's the big deal?"

"The big deal is that I wanted to show you something. And I would rather not get interrupted by Harry's magic.

"Oh really? What is it? What do you want to show me?"

Honey smiled. "It's probably the most special . . . special whatchamacallit in the whole world."

"A whatchamacallit?" Becky laughed. "Sounds like you don't even know what it is, so how can it be so special?"

"I do so know what it is. I just can't say yet. It'll spoil the surprise. I invited Claire and Isabela over too, and I want to wait for them."

Becky sat on Honey's bed. "All right, but now you got me really wondering."

"ABRACADABRA!"

Honey clenched her teeth. "Ugh." She looked through her bedroom window, hoping to see Isabela and Claire running toward her house. But no, not yet. Honey looked past the giant oak tree in her front yard, over the neighborhood roofs, over the tree tops toward Folly Farm—one of the many places in Sleepy Hollow that made Honey cringe. Folly Farm was home to Mayor Maximus Kligore and his three kids. It was because of Mayor Kligore that Sleepy Hollow had been plunged into a state of forever Halloween. More to the point, it was because of the mayor's dark magic. And that frightened Honey.

"It's still raining," Honey said. Honey grabbed her turtle-shaped backpack. It was neon green with googly eyes. It had been a Christmas gift from her mom. The turtle made her feel secure—especially on stormy nights.

3

"Good old Sleepy Hollow," Becky said. "It's kinda icky every single day."

But when you lived in a town where every day was Halloween night, rain and wind and gray clouds were pretty much the norm—unless of course Mayor Kligore decided sunshine was in order. Then he would simply cast one of his magic spells and poof—sunshine. The mayor controlled everything in Sleepy Hollow—the weather, the newspaper, and even birthdays, sometimes. Not everybody in town knew this about the mayor—but Honey did. So did Harry; it was why he practiced his magic so much. Harry was often called upon to use his Deep Magic against Mayor Kligore's dark magic. And, at least for now, Harry always won. Yep, her brother Harry Moon was something special. But sometimes, like today, Honey wanted people to think she was something special also.

"Aww come on," Becky said. "Show me the whatchamacallit. Claire is always late, and she's probably making Isabela late too."

"All right," Honey said. "I keep it hidden."

4

Honey slipped the backpack over the chair. "I'll get it."

"Oh goodie," Becky said. "I'm so excited to see it."

"Honey." It was her mom calling up the stairs before Honey could get the whatchamacallit. "Claire and Isabela are here. I'm sending them up."

Honey dashed to the bedroom door. "Okay, Mom, thanks."

"Oh good," Becky said, clapping her hands. "We're all here. I'm so excited."

Claire burst into the room. "Hey, what's up?"

"Hi," Isabela said, following right behind, "we came right away. Your text sounded urgent. What's go—" She stopped in mid-sentence. Her eyes grew big. "Becky! Your hair. Where did your curls go?"

Becky pushed a few stray strands behind

5

her ear. "I finally talked my mom into letting me straighten it. Like it?"

Isabela smiled. "Yes, it looks great, but I liked your curls too."

"Oh, c'mon," Claire said. "Hair schmair. I'm sure that's not why Honey called us all over here." She flopped onto Honey's bed and grabbed a softball glove from a nearby shelf. "Great glove, Honey. If you ever want to sell it—"

"No, hair is not why she called us here," Becky said. "Honey has a whatchamacallit to show us."

"Whatchamacallit?" Isabela said with a bit of song in her voice. "I'm afraid I don't know that word."

"Oh," Becky said. "It's a word we Americans use when we don't know the real name."

Isabela's brow wrinkled.

Honey smiled and looked at her friends. "I

do so know its real name. I just didn't want to give it away until everybody was here."

"ABRACADABRA!"

"That does it." Honey grimaced. "I'm gonna tell him to knock it off." She marched across the hall and banged on Harry's door. "HARROLD MOON! Open this door right *now!*" A few seconds later, the door opened, and there stood Harry wearing his magic cape. Harry was short for his age, so he and Honey were pretty much the same height. She looked him squarely in the eyes. "Knock it off, Harry! I have guests."

"Knock what off?" Harry asked.

"The abracadabra stuff. I have friends over."

"Oooooo, right away," Harry said. "I wasn't aware Your Highness was entertaining." And then he bowed.

"Come on, Harry, please."

"Oh all right," Harry said. "I was about to get something to eat anyway."

When Honey got back to her room, Claire was still lying on her bed tossing a ball in the air and catching it in Honey's glove. Honey caught Becky sneaking a peek in one of

Honey's desk drawers.

"Hey," Honey said. "It's not in there. I keep

it in a very special place."

"I can't imagine what it is," Isabela said.

Honey reached over Claire's head and snagged a book—*Alice In Wonderland*.

"It's just a book," Claire said. "Big deal."

"Well, it's a very good book," Isabela said.

"No, no." Honey sat at her desk and opened the book. "This is just its hiding place."

"What is it?" Becky asked as Honey removed a silver necklace from its secret hiding place. "I can't stand the suspense."

"It's a necklace," Isabela said. "It's very pretty."

Honey held the necklace so her friends could all see. "It's more than a necklace. It's a locket. And it's very, very old—antique. It's also a Moon family heirloom. And that makes it even more special." She set the delicate, round locket on her palm. "See, it's silver and has a moon face. And look at all these pretty grape leaves etched around the circumference."

"Well, the moon face certainly makes sense," Claire said, "since your name is Moon and all. Not sure about the grape leaves, though."

Honey opened the delicate case. Inside was a picture of a man. An old man with a long gray beard. His hair was spikey like Harry's.

10   "Wow," Isabela said, "Who is that?"

"I'll tell you the whole story in a sec. Help me clasp it."

Becky clasped the necklace around Honey's neck. Honey admired it in her mirror. "Don't you just love it? Have you ever seen anything so amazing and old at the same time?"

"It sure is," Becky said. "I've never seen anything like it."

"That's because it's a family heirloom. Heirlooms are often one-of-a-kind. The man in the picture is my great-great-grandfather, Astronomer Moon. He's really important to the Moon family and to Sleepy Hollow."

"Wow," Becky said. "What a great name. Can I try it on?"

"In a second," Honey said still admiring herself.

"So, what's the story?" Isabela asked.

11

"Well, you see, Astronomer Moon was an archaeologist, always traveling around discovering and digging up things—artifacts and junk. My great-great-grandmother missed him a lot, so he gave her this moon locket to help her feel a little better. And now it's an heirloom. My grandma gave it to my mom when she married my dad and became a Moon."

"Sweet," Claire said. "I think that's the first bona fide heirloom I've ever seen. My mother has this raggedy, old quilt she says is an heirloom. I think it just smells funny." Claire held her nose.

"Please, Honey, let me try it on," Becky said.

"Okay." Honey unclasped the necklace and was just about to put it around Becky's neck when she heard her mother. "Honey, I have laundry."

Honey quickly put the necklace back into the book and slammed it closed.

The door flew open. Mary Moon held a basket of Honey's clothes. "Sorry to interrupt," she said. "Honey please put these clothes away. All of them. In drawers and not on your floor." She set the basket down.

"Sure, Mom," Honey said. "I'll do it."

"Okay," Mary said. "Don't have to do it right away. But soon."

Honey waited until her mother was gone and said, "Phew, that was close."

"Why did you hide it?" Becky asked.

Honey opened the book and removed the locket. She let the chain dangle through her fingers. "Real silver feels so nice."

"Yeah, why *did* you hide it?" Claire asked. "Aren't you allowed to have the locket?"

"Sure," Honey said. "It's just that it's so precious and so special, my mother doesn't like me flaunting it. That's all."

Honey saw Becky's eyebrows rise.

13

Isabela said, "Oh, okay, I guess."

Claire went back to tossing the ball in the air and staring at Honey. "I'm thinking your mom doesn't know you have it and that you would get in trouble if your mom knew."

"So let me try it on now," Becky said, ignoring Claire's remark.

Honey placed the necklace inside the book again and returned it to the bookshelf. "Maybe another time. Let's go get a snack."

"Now that's what I'm talkin' about," Claire said. "I could go for some cookies and milk."

"Me too," Isabela said. "I skipped lunch today."

Honey grabbed Becky's hand. "Come on, I'll let you try it on later."

"Don't forget," Becky said.

Before she turned off the bedroom light, Honey caught a glimpse of Turtle. He was kind of staring back at her. "I know," Honey whispered. "That *was* a close call."

Honey turned off the light and pulled the door closed.

FRIED PLANTAINS

"To the kitchen!" Honey said. "The cookies await."

They headed down the steps and met Harry on his way up. He was balancing a glass of milk on a plate of cookies.

"Hi, Harry," Becky said as Claire and Isabela squeezed past him and almost made him spill.

"How's it going?"

"Great," Harry said, turning sideways and trying to squeeze past the girls. "Where's the fire?"

"No fire," Honey said. "We're after some of those cookies. I hope you didn't eat them all, *Harrold*. Now if you'll let us get past, please."

"Good idea," Harry said. "Mom made oatmeal raisin and chocolate chip. I think all the chocolate chips are on my plate. I may have left a few oatmeal ones. I don't remember."

"Have another magic show coming up?" Becky asked. She smiled, and Honey shivered as she was pretty sure she caught a sparkle in Becky's eyes.

"Yep," Harry said. "I'm doing a bar mitzvah."

"Cool," Becky said. "I bet you'll do great, Harry. Your magic is incredible."

Honey grabbed Becky's hand. "The cookies?

16

Remember?"

Harry stepped aside and let the girls pass.

Claire and Isabela were already in the kitchen. Claire was munching on a cookie. "Your mom makes the best," she said through a mouthful.

"Come on, sit down," Mary Moon said. "I have plenty. Made four dozen today."

"That's enough for me," Honey said.

1]

"Thank you, Mrs. Moon," Isabela said. "In Ecuador, we don't eat oatmeal cookies. We eat patacones."

"Ohh," Mary said. "What is that?"

"Fried plantains. They're delicious."

"You mean like bananas?" Honey said.

Claire snorted and almost spat her oatmeal cookie across the room when she laughed. "Fried bananas? That's weird."

Isabela smiled. "Oatmeal cookies? That's weird."

"Well," Mary Moon said, "here's something I'm sure you'll all agree on." She filled three tall tumblers with milk. "I'll be in the laundry room if you need me."

"Never be afraid to try new food," Isabela said.

18

Becky swallowed and said, "Don't forget to let me try on—"

Honey kicked her under the table before she could finish her sentence. "Ouch" Becky said as she reached down and rubbed her shin. "You didn't have to kick me."

"I just don't want my mom to hear."

"Okay, okay, just don't kick me anymore."

"Hey," Isabela said. "It's almost three o'clock. I need to go. I have to walk Bart, and I promised Grace I'd clean up my room."

"Awww, really?" Honey said. "But we're having so much fun."

"I know." Isabela pushed her chair in. "But I really have to go."

"Hey," Honey said. "I have a brilliant idea. Why don't we have a sleepover?"

She called to her mom, "Is it okay, Mom? Can we have a sleepover?"

"Please, Mrs. Moon," Becky called.

Mary Moon walked out of the laundry room carrying a pile of towels. "Sure. I think that's a fine idea."

"Yayyy," Becky said. "I just have to ask my mom."

"I need to ask my dad," Claire said. "But I'm sure it will be all right. I'll just text him now."

"I'll ask Grace," Isabela said. "But I'm sure she'll say yes."

"Great," Honey said. "Come back right after supper. Claire can just eat with us." Honey looked at her mom. "Okay, Mom?"

"Sure, nothing fancy, though, tonight. Salad and sloppy joes on whole wheat buns."

"Sounds great, Mrs. Moon," Claire said. "And Dad just texted back. "He said okay, but I should run home and get my sleeping bag."

"Oh, that's right," Isabela said. "I don't have a sleeping bag."

"No problem." Honey bit into another cookie. "You can use Harry's."

Claire laughed. "Yuck. Probably smells like a hamster cage."

⌇

After supper, Honey and Claire loaded the dishwasher and cleaned up the kitchen without being asked.

FRIED PLANTAINS

"Thank you, girls," Mary Moon said. "Now, how about I rustle up some healthy snacks for tonight's sleepover?"

"Okay, Mom," Honey said. "But not too healthy. Maybe toss in some chips. We're going to watch a movie later."

"Oh, which one?" Mary asked.

"I was thinking Legend of Sleepy Hollow," Claire said. "It's on Mayor Kligore's required movie viewing list." She laughed. "I don't think Isabela has seen it yet."

21

Honey sighed. "Awww, that movie is all right, but I get so sick of Halloween and that silly Headless Horseman."

"I know you do," Claire said, "but the rest of us like it. It's what makes Sleepy Hollow so special."

"I know, I know." Honey finished drying her hands. "Let's go get into out pj's before Isabela and Becky get here."

Before she did anything else, Honey checked on the necklace. It was still there, snug between pages thirteen and fourteen.

"I don't believe you," Claire said as she slipped into a long nightgown.

"Believe me about what?"

"That necklace. I think you're tricking us."

"I am not. It's just too special to leave lying around in the open. You can never tell in Sleepy Hollow. Strange things are always happening."

Claire ran her fingers through her hair. "Right, like Mayor Kligore wants your necklace."

Honey touched the ornate moon face. "You never know. It is special."

They had just gotten changed and were on the steps when the doorbell rang.

"They're here," Claire said. "Now we can get this party started."

"Roger that, Claire," Honey said.

Honey pulled open the door. Isabela and Becky were there holding sleeping bags and wearing their pj's under their raincoats. "Hey, thought you didn't have a sleeping bag," Honey said to Isabela.

"I didn't, but Grace let me use hers. She said she'll buy me one soon. And it smells better than a hamster cage."

"Good-o," Honey said. "Come on in. We'll set up in the living room."

That was when she saw Harry flop on the couch and grab the remote.

"Hey," Honey said. "You need to leave. We have the living room for the night, and we're watching a movie. Sleepover."

"Aww, come on," Harry said. "It's not like you own the place."

"Tonight, she does—sort of," said Honey's dad. He was standing near the den. "Come on, Harry. I owe you a chess do-over."

"Oh, all right," Harry said. "But I'm not holding back this time."

"No magic tricks," John Moon said as Harry

walked into the den.

"Great," Honey said. "They're gone. Just set your sleeping bags wherever. Probably in front of the TV for the movie. Mom's making snacks, and she's already got a fire going.

"Oh, I just love fireplaces," Isabela said. "They make everything so cozy."

That was when Half Moon sauntered in, circled a few times and flopped on the hearth, tucking every one of his four legs comfortably underneath his body.

25

"Hey, girls only," Honey said. "Get out of here, Half. Go find Harry."

"Aww, it's all right," Isabela said. "I like your dog."

"Fine," Honey said. "But if he farts, he's out."

The girls unrolled their sleeping bags. Honey

was still using the same bag she used when she was a little kid. The one with cartoon images of the Headless Horseman all over it. "I think I need a new, more mature bag."

Claire's sleeping bag looked like it had seen more than its fair share of camping trips. "Look at this," she said pointing to the bottom corner of the green nylon bag. "Remember when it caught on fire on the Mummy Mates trip?"

Honey laughed. "Yeah, that was so funny."

"Funny?" Becky said. "That trip was a disaster. I still remember the seed ticks and the storm and the flash flood."

"Wow," Isabela said. "Sounds awful."

"Aww, it was at the time," Honey said. "But we made it out alive, and we all got our hiking patches."

"Well, we're safe in your house tonight." Isabela unrolled her sleeping bag.

"Right-o," Claire said. "Nothing can get us tonight. Turn on the movie."

When Honey grabbed the DVD from the bookshelf, she spotted Harry peeking in from the den.

"Were you eavesdropping, Harry?" she called.

"Me? Of course not." Then he laughed. "At least not yet."

27

Honey didn't like the sound of that.

28

SLEEPOVER SHENANIGANS

"This is my first sleepover ever," Isabela said.

Becky wiggled into her sleeping bag. Her bag was purple with fancy unicorns. "Really? Don't they have sleepovers in Ecuador?"

Isabela unzipped her bag. "I guess, but my parents died before I could have one, and I didn't have many friends in foster care."

Honey couldn't imagine what it would be like to lose her parents. But she was certain that she would probably think about them a million times a day if she did. Sometimes, she could tell when Isabela was thinking about her mother and father. Isabela would get a kind of faraway look in her eyes and sometimes wipe away a tear. Honey smiled into Isabela's glistening eyes. "I'm glad you're here."

30

"Well, now you're adopted," Claire said.

"And we're your friends," Becky added.

"And I'm sure Grace will let you have sleepovers." Honey said.

"I know." Isabela wiggled into her sleeping bag. "She's so nice." Half Moon moved off the hearth and snuggled at Isabela's feet.

Come on," Claire said. "Let's watch the movie."

Honey grabbed the remote from the coffee table. "Okay. You're gonna love it, Isabela. I've seen it like nine times."

"I thought you hated Halloween," Isabela said.

"I do," Honey said. "But the movie is a classic. *The Legend of Sleepy Hollow.* Mayor Kligore wants everyone to see it—it's kind of his movie."

Honey opened the DVD case. "Mom said she'll bring us some snacks."

31

"Ugh," Claire said. "I hope she has chips. Your mom always makes us healthy junk like carrot sticks and celery."

Honey was just about to put the DVD into the player when Harry bopped into the living room wearing his cape and carrying his magic top hat. "Hey," he said. "How about some magic, girls?"

"Nooooo, Harry!" Honey said. "Not now. We're watching a movie."

"Aww, come on," Harry said. "I need to practice in front of an audience."

"It's all right with me," Becky said. "I'd like to see some magic."

"Of course, *you* would," Honey said with a little snark in her voice.

"Yeah, me too," Isabela said.

"I'm in," Claire said.

Honey let out a heavy sigh. "Oh, all right, but only a few tricks, Harry. This is a girls' night."

"Great," Harry said. "I really appreciate this."

He started the show with some pretty routine card tricks and sleight of hand marvels. Isabela especially liked it when he made the ace of hearts appear inside Becky's sleeping bag, and then he made a rope that was cut into four pieces fall back together and wiggle around on the floor like a snake.

"And now for the best act of the evening," Harry said. "I need a volunteer from the audience."

Becky's hand shot straight up. "Me, pick me."

"Thank you, Miss Becky, will you join me on the stage?"

Honey laughed. "Stage. Come on. You're standing on a throw rug."

Harry smiled. "Now, just wait here, Becky. I need to get the Amazing Disappearing Box."

"Okay," Becky said. "I'll wait right here for you to come back."

"Disappearing?" Isabela said. "Is he gonna make Becky disappear?"

"Probably," Claire said. "But it's just a trick. An illusion."

"I know," Isabela said. "But it's still pretty neat."

"I happen to know how he does all of his tricks," Honey said. "But I've been sworn to secrecy under penalty of being forced to smell Harry's sneakers."

"Ewwwww, gross," Claire said.

Harry pushed a tall rectangular box on wheels into the living room. It was painted bluish-gray, like the sky at twilight, and there were gold moons all over it.

Harry bowed. "And now, as you can see, this is an ordinary box." He tapped the sides and spun it around. He opened the door and tapped the walls inside. "No trap doors. Nothing tricky. Just a solid pine box."

"Ugh," Claire said. "Don't they make coffins out of pine?"

"Good old Sleepy Hollow," Honey said.

"And now, Becky, if you'll just step into the box."

"Okay, Harry," Becky said.

As Becky stepped inside, Honey noticed Harry whisper in her ear.

"Ah ha!" Honey said. "You just told her what to do."

"No, he didn't," Becky said, glaring at her friend. "No, he did not, Honey."

"Becky," Harry said, "just stand still right there in the box and don't be frightened and don't do anything."

Harry closed the door.

"And now, ladies, and Honey," Harry said, "I will send Becky to the great beyond."

He waved his cape in front of the box. Then he spun it around three times and tapped on it three times with his magic wand.

"ABRACADABRA."

Harry spun the box around one more time and opened the door. Becky was gone.

Claire and Isabela applauded.

"That's *impossible*, Harry! *WHERE IS BECKY?*" Claire asked with a yell.

"Yeah, yeah, great trick," Honey said. "Now bring her back so we can watch our movie."

36

"That was incredible, Harry," Isabela said. "Where'd she go?"

"To the great beyond," Harry said. "And now I will bring her back."

Harry waved his cape in front of the box. Then he spun it around three times. He tapped on it three times and said, *"ABRACADABRA."*

He opened the door, and Becky was *still* gone. "Uh oh," said Harry, scratching his head looking into the empty box.

Honey laughed. "Well done, Moondini. Your

trick didn't work. So where exactly is my friend?"

"I-I-I don't understand," Harry said. "I must have done something wrong." He spun the box around again and tapped on it three times. He opened the door, and Becky was still gone. "Mmm. I wonder what is happening."

"MOM! Harrold has lost Becky, and he's ruining my sleepover!" Honey hollered.

"Well, she has to be around here somewhere," Claire said. "We know this is a trick. Let's find her."

They searched everywhere. Harry even checked in Harvest's room. Honey practically tore the den apart, and Claire checked outside while Isabel checked the kitchen and the garage.

"I wonder where she is?" Harry asked. "This has never happened before."

"Maybe you're more powerful than you think," Isabela said.

37

"Uhm, maybe," Harry said.

A few minutes later, Becky walked into the room. "Hey, Harry!" she said. "You never brought me back from the great beyond. How long do you want me to wait out there?" The girls ran to Becky and gave her a group hug.

"I tried to," Harry said. "What happened?"

Becky shrugged. "I guess the great beyond was a little farther away than we knew."

"Well, I'm glad you're back," Honey said. "Now that your best attempt to ruin my sleepover has failed, please leave, Harry. We have a movie to watch."

Harry packed up his magic gear and bowed in front of the girls. "Well, thanks for being such a great audience," he said as he pushed the disappearing box into the den.

Becky slid the DVD into the player and turned on the TV. Then the girls all slipped into their sleeping bags just as Mary Moon came into the living room with a big bowl of popcorn. "Here you go, girls," she said. "Popcorn and apple slices."

"Oh, yummy," Claire said.

"And I even fried some bananas," Mary Moon said. "I didn't have any plantains, but I thought bananas would work in a pinch.

"Ohhh, *gracias*," Isabela said.

"Let me try some," Claire said.

Mary set the goodies on the coffee table and headed upstairs. "Good night, girls."

"Good night," they called.

Claire bit into the fried banana chip. "Hey, that's not bad. Not bad at all."

The movie started. "Okay," Honey said. "Finally. It's just us."

39

But the movie had barely gotten though the opening credits when Becky jumped up. "Ohhhh, what is it. I am sooo itchy." She was scratching all over. "My legs and arms." She was dancing around and scratching.

"Well, it can't be seed ticks," Claire said, "like on the camping trip."

"Is it something you ate?" Isabela asked. "Maybe the fried bananas."

40

All Becky could do was shake her head and scratch.

That was when Honey heard laughter coming from the den. "HARRY, WHAT DID YOU DO?" Honey screamed. "That brother of mine. He's behind this. He's playing tricks on us."

Claire opened Becky's sleeping bag while Becky was busy dancing around like a whirling dervish, scratching at her legs, and Half Moon barked like mad.

"What is that?" Isabela asked. She pointed

at grayish powder all over the inside of Becky's sleeping bag.

"Itching powder," Honey said. "My numskull brother put itching powder in your sleeping bag."

"Ohhh, make it stop," Becky said. "I'm so itchy."

Honey dashed to the stairs. "Moooooom-mmmmm," she called. "We need you."

Claire was busy laughing. "Way to go Harry."

"Don't laugh," Becky cried. "This itching is really bad. And I thought Harry liked me."

Claire hunkered into her sleeping bag. "He does. That's why he—" This time Claire screamed. "What's in my bag? Something slimy!" Claire wiggled around in her sleeping bag, and with another scream, she pulled out a slimy fake snake.

Isabela and Honey laughed.

Claire tossed the snake across the room. "Now that's not funny. I *hate* snakes." Half Moon ran after the snake.

Mary Moon was standing near the steps, her eyes wide. "What on earth is going on?"

"Harry!" Honey said. "He put itching powder in Becky's sleeping bag. And a fake snake in Claire's. He is wrecking my sleepover."

42

"Oh, dear," Mary Moon said with a little chuckle. "That Harry." She walked to Becky and said, "Come on, dear. Let's get you washed up while Honey and Claire and Isabela shake out your bag."

"All right, Mom," Honey said.

"Take it outside," Mary Moon said as a reminder.

"Yes, Mrs. Moon," Isabela said. Then she whispered to Honey, "You know, it is kind of funny."

"I'll get him," Honey said. "Harry Moon will pay for what he did."

44

Gone Missing

Morning finally came, and Honey awakened to the luscious aroma of bacon, waffles, and what she was pretty certain was strawberries. She nudged Becky, who had finally gotten to sleep after the itching-powder incident. "Wake up, Becky. It's morning."

Becky sat straight up like she had found a

snake in her sleeping bag. "What? What is it?"

"Morning," Honey said. "We made it through with no jokes from Harry."

Isabela was next to rise. "Good morning," she said with a yawn. "Everyone still here?"

"Yep," Honey said. "No more jokes."

Claire, who could sleep through an earth-quake, didn't budge. She didn't budge even after Honey bopped her with a pillow. She didn't budge even after Isabela shook her arm. She didn't budge until Becky gave her huge shove and said, "Claire! Wake up!"

Claire wiggled from her sleeping bag, scrubbing the sleep from her eyes. "What gives? It's Sunday. A day of rest."

"Come on," Honey said. "I smell strawberries and waffles."

"Oh, boy," Becky said. "I love strawberries and waffles."

46

"Well, I hope there's whipped cream," Claire said. "I'll get out of bed for whipped cream."

"Me too," Isabela said.

Honey was first to the kitchen.

"Smells good, Mom," she said.

"Good morning," Mary Moon said. "Come in girls and have a seat. Breakfast is just about ready."

47

"I can't wait," Claire said. "Is there whipped cream?"

Mary Moon laughed. "Certainly, Claire, and maple syrup if you want."

The table was already set with pretty plates and small glasses of orange juice and cloth napkins.

"Wow, Mom," Honey said. "It's all so fancy. You didn't have to make a big fuss."

Mary smiled. "Oh, I just think it's nice to fancy things up sometimes."

"Thank you," Isabela said. "I feel like royalty."

"Yeah, pretty neat," Claire said. "We just use paper towels for napkins at our house."

Honey nudged Claire. "So do we a lot of the time. But this is nice."

48

"It sure is," Becky said. "And I am so hungry I think I can eat six waffles."

"Be ready in a few minutes," Mary Moon said.

Isabela leaned toward Honey and whispered, "I have an idea."

"About what?" Honey said.

"To get back at Harry. Follow me. But grab the syrup first."

Honey sneaked the bottle of Mrs.

Butterworth's inside her bathrobe. She and Isabela chuckled as they headed upstairs. "What's your plan?" Honey asked.

"Harry's bathroom," Isabela said. "Do you have a shampoo bottle that's pretty much empty?"

Honey opened the linen closet door. "Yeah, Mom keeps them for emergencies." She grabbed a tall, plastic bottle. "Now what?"

"Perfect," Isabela said. "Pour the syrup into the shampoo bottle and then replace it with the shampoo in the bathroom for Harry."

Honey snickered. "Ohhh, this is gonna be great."

Honey dumped some of the maple syrup into the shampoo bottle. She sneaked it into the bathroom and managed to replace the real shampoo seconds before she heard Harry come out of his bedroom. He was headed for the bathroom.

"Come on," Isabela said. "Just act cool."

They smiled all the way back to the kitchen.

"Where were you two?" Becky asked.

"Yeah," Claire said. "What gives?"

"You'll see," Honey said. "Be cool."

"Mysterious," Claire said. "Well, right now I am so hungry I think I could eat a hundred waffles."

Mary placed a plate of waffles stacked six high on the table. "Just start with one," she said. "They're pretty big."

"They look delicious, Mrs. Moon," Isabela said with a giggle. "Really sweet."

Honey had just spooned some strawberries onto her waffle when Harry came screaming into the kitchen.

"*WHO DID THIS?* Look at my hair. It won't

wash out. I smell like maple syrup."

Honey burst into laughter when she saw Harry with his already spiky dark hair sticking straight up like black stalagmites.

"What happened?" Becky asked.

"Somebody put maple syrup in the shampoo bottle." Harry's face grew red.

"Oh, dear." Mary Moon hid a smile. "That's terrible." She barely got the words out because even she couldn't help but chuckle at Harry's sticky misfortune.

"Who did it?" Harry demanded.

"We all did. To get you back for last night," Honey said.

Harry laughed. "Oh, yeah, last night. Guess you found the snake and the itching powder. I *am* a genius."

"I didn't think it was very funny," Becky said. She scratched her neck. Then she laughed and pointed at Harry. "But *this* is really funny."

Mary Moon refilled Claire's orange juice glass. "Uhm, I think the winner of this battle is the maple syrup. Now that's genius."

Harry made a loud harrumph noise. "This isn't over!" And then he stormed out of the kitchen while the girls all laughed and high-fived.

"Okay, okay, settle down, girls," Mary said. "Your folks are coming to pick you up, and then it's off to church for you, Honey Moon."

"Right, Mom," Honey said.

"Okay," Becky said. "Guess I'll see you later, Harry."

Honey and her friends straightened up the living room and rolled their sleeping bags, which they left near the front door. They changed into their daytime clothes and waited.

"Hey," Isabela said. "Becky never got to try on the locket."

"Oh yeah," Honey said. "I guess we have time. Let's go to my room."

But Becky jumped up quickly. "Oh, no, that's okay. I think I hear my mom's car."

She ran to the door. "Yep, she's here! See you later." Becky snatched up her gear and flew out the door in a rush.

"That was weird," Claire said.

"It sure was," Honey said. "I didn't hear a car pull into the driveway."

"Yeah," Claire said. "It's like she still has itching powder all over her."

A few minutes later, Isabela and Claire were gone, and Honey was alone in her bedroom getting ready for the day.

54

After making sure she had *real* shampoo, Honey showered and dressed. She chose her pretty lilac dress with the tiny yellow flowers. It was a nice spring dress even though it was still pouring rain and felt more like autumn.

As she was checking things out in the mirror Honey thought, *Hmm, I bet the locket would look perfect with this dress. I'll just give it a try.*

She pulled *Alice in Wonderland* from the shelf and opened it. But the locket was gone.

"That's strange," she whispered. "I know I put it back here. Where is it?" Honey shook the book. She searched the other books on her shelf. She searched under her bed. She searched on her bed and in all her drawers as she grew more and more frantic.

"This is terrible," she whimpered with tears welling up in her eyes. "Where can it be?" She looked at Turtle. "I'm in trouble now, Turtle. Do you know where it is?" Turtle didn't say a word. He just looked at her with his big googly eyes.

Then she remembered Harry's breakfast promise. "Harry Moon! He took it."

Honey dashed across the hall to Harry's room. He was busy trying to comb the stickiness out of his hair. "Please leave. I'm trying to get this comb through my hair, which is pretty tough since it's all stuck together," he said. "And what are you doing in my room, anyway?"

"Harry," Honey said. "Hand it over."

"Hand what over?"

"My necklace. The moon locket."

Harry's eye's widened. "What are you talking about?"

"The family heirloom. You know, the locket with Astronomer Moon's picture inside."

Harry looked in his mirror. He was not happy with the way his hair was glued together. "Oh, that. I haven't seen that since the last time Mom wore it. At Christmas."

Honey sat on Harry's bed and dropped her face into her hands. "Oh, wow. I'm in really big trouble."

"What did you do?"

"Look, promise not to tell."

"Maybe," Harry said. "Just tell me. Did you lose Mom's locket?"

Honey nodded her head like a bobble doll. "I think so. Maybe. I mean, I'm not sure."

"It would be better if you made sense. Start from the beginning."

Honey let out a sigh that seemed to come from deep inside. "I took the necklace from Mom's jewelry box. Just to try it. I mean I don't think it's fair that she'll give the locket to your wife someday. I just wanted a chance to wear it."

57

"Silly," Harry said. "I'm pretty sure Mom will give you lots of chances to wear it before that happens."

"Well, we all know you want Sarah Sinclair to end up with it one day."

Harry smiled. "I hope so. But tell me the story."

"Anyway, I was showing it to Becky and Claire and Isabela yesterday. I didn't want Mom to know I had it, so I hid it inside a book. And

when I went to get it just now . . . to put it back
. . . it's totally gone. I searched my whole room.
I can't find it. Help me, Harry. Please."

Harry took a deep breath. "I can help you
look, but—"

"Don't you have some special magic to get
lost things back?"

"I wish," Harry said. "Then I'd still have my
Xbox controller and about a dozen baseball
cards."

Honey swiped a few tears from her eyes.
"Mom'll kill me."

"No, she won't kill you. But she will ground
you. Forever!"

"Where can it be, Harry? *Where?*"

A PLAN MOST DISASTROUS

oney wanted to stay home and search for the locket, but she had to go to church. It was not a good time. She couldn't concentrate on anything Reverend McAdams was saying. All she wanted to do was get home and look for the locket. She also kind of wanted to tell her mother what she had done—but no, she kept pushing that thought out of her mind. The locket was sure to turn up. And then she would never ever borrow it again.

Honey was anxious to get home, but it was kind of a Moon family tradition that they went to Saywells Drugstore for lunch on Sundays.

"Can I just go home, Mom?" Honey asked.

"Why, you love Saywells," Mary Moon said.

"I know. I just don't feel well."

60

"Too many waffles," John Moon said. "Just come along. You can watch us eat." Then he laughed.

Mary Moon felt Honey's forehead. "No fever. Come along. You're probably overtired from the sleepover."

Having a nurse for a mom made it awfully difficult to get away with pretending to be sick.

So off she went to Saywells. She managed to get through the lunch okay, but the instant she got home, Honey raced to her room, changed into her regular clothes, and resumed her search.

She searched everywhere—even Harvest's room and the garage. The locket was just nowhere to be found. And she kept getting more and more upset.

Honey ended her search in her room. She looked inside *Alice in Wonderland*, hoping it might have reappeared. It hadn't. Now she knew for certain that the precious family heirloom had, like Alice, fallen down a rabbit hole.

With even darker clouds moving over Sleepy Hollow and rain still pouring, Honey could only come to one conclusion. The locket had been stolen. But by whom?

Honey didn't want to think about it. The possibilities were just too horrible to consider. The only people who even knew she had the locket were Becky, Isabela, and Claire. *Is it possible that one of my friends has taken it?*

She sat at her desk, looking out over the dark town and came up with a plan. Maybe she could replace it.

With a renewed energy, Honey dashed down the steps and into the den. Half Moon followed her. She found a box of old family photos. She wanted to find a picture of the locket. She knew some pictures were taken of her mom wearing it on very special occasions. But she would also need a photo of Astronomer Moon, and they were pretty rare. The only one she knew of was the one in the locket.

She had a lot of photos scattered on the den floor when her mom came into the room. "Oh, there you are," she said. "I was looking all over. What are you doing?"

Honey swallowed. Her palms grew sweaty. "Oh—oh nothing, Mom. I just got to thinking about family history and stuff and thought I'd look through these pictures," she lied.

"How sweet," Mary Moon said. "I wish I could look through them with you, but the hospital called. I need to go in for a couple of hours. Your dad is outside working on his car, and Harvest is with him. The rain has finally stopped so your dad wanted to take advantage."

"Okay, Mom, see you later."

"Astronomer Moon," Mary said.

Honey gasped and then looked up at her mom. "What?"

"Astronomer Moon. He's the guy in the photo under Half's tail." Half Moon barked once and wagged his tail at the sound of his name and sent the picture flying across the room.

"Sorry," Honey said.

"Yes, be careful with that one. It's the only one besides the one in the heirloom."

Honey's eyes grew wide. She looked straight at her mom like she was expecting her to say she knew what Honey did. Why else would she mention the locket?

Mary Moon chuckled. "I really need to put that picture in a frame. See you later."

Honey waited a few moments until she heard the front door close. She grabbed the picture of Astronomer Moon. "This is him, Half. It kind of looks like the picture in the locket. I think his beard is longer in this picture though."

Honey looked through the photographs until she found a picture of her mother wearing the locket. "Perfect."

Half Moon let out two loud barks.

"I'll make this okay, Half," Honey said. "You'll see."

Honey gathered all the photos into the box and replaced it on the shelf. She grabbed her raincoat and slid the pictures into her pocket. Then, she ran out to the garage to see her dad. He had his head under the hood of his little green sports car. The car had a name. Emma. John Moon loved that car and took very good care of it. He always seemed to be tinkering with it though, even when it wasn't broken.

"Hey, Dad," Honey said. "Would it be okay if I went down to Magic Row for a while? I just want to look around."

John pulled his head out from under the hood. Unfortunately, he banged it on the way. "Ouch," he said rubbing his noggin. "That really hurt."

65

Honey laughed a little. So did Harvest. This was nothing new. Her dad often banged his head on the hood.

"Sure," he said. "But not too late. And I don't think you need that rain coat anymore."

"You can never tell," Honey said. "Could start up again." She wheeled her bike from the garage. "This will be faster."

Honey slipped her backpack over her shoulders, but just as she was about to jump on her bike, she heard her father calling.

"Honey, I almost forgot to tell you something."

Honey wheeled her bike onto the driveway.

"What's that, Dad?"

"Your mom wanted me to remind you that we are going to the annual Nurses' Gala at the hospital Friday night. So, you and Harry will need to babysit Harvest."

Honey climbed onto her bike. "The Nurses' Gala. That's the one where you guys get all dressed up in gowns and tuxedos?"

"That's the one," John Moon said. "Fancy dancy."

"No problem," Honey said. But her mind was definitely elsewhere as she pushed off toward Magic Row.

68

FALL IN LINE

oney checked again that the pictures were still in her coat pocket. This whole thing was making her a nervous wreck. She took off down the street. She rode through a few puddles on her way and splashed her coat.

She peddled straight to Jinx Jewelry Store on Magic Row. Because of the number of tourists in and out of Sleepy Hollow, most of the stores stayed open on Sundays. The town was a national attraction. Everyone wanted to come to a place where it was Halloween every day. The stores made a lot of money, and of course, a nice piece of the profits went straight to Mayor Kligore, who claimed to use it to make Sleepy Hollow even more spectacular.

Honey checked for the photos again and was just about to enter the store when her phone jingled. It was Claire. Her first thought was to answer it and come right out and ask Claire if she swiped the locket, but then she decided not to. Accusing friends of stealing was not an easy thing to do. And besides, Claire would be more likely to swipe Honey's baseball glove before she'd swipe the necklace. But still, Honey did not feel like talking.

Honey went into the store. The owner, Jeremiah Jinx, was behind the counter helping another customer. Honey looked at the jewelry items while she waited, hoping that Mr. Jinx would hurry.

Finally, the other customer left, and Honey

stepped up to the counter. "Hi, Mr. Jinx."

"Well, hello there, Honey Moon. What brings you to the jewelry store?"

Jeremiah Jinx was a nice man. He had a balding head and bushy eyebrows. His nose was rather long, and he was wearing a striped tie over a gray shirt.

Honey sighed and pulled the photos from her backpack. Then she told Mr. Jinx the whole story. "I was wondering if you could replace it."

"Oh, dear," Mr. Jinx said. "I know that locket. It's very, very old. Very old indeed. I've repaired it on a few occasions, so I know how special it is to your mama. It could never be replaced. At least not easily."

Honey felt tears well in her eyes.

"I'm sorry, Honey," Mr. Jinx said. "Perhaps it would be best if you just told your mother the truth. She'll understand. Honesty is the best policy, as they say."

Honey wiped tears from her cheeks. "Thank you. I guess that's what I'll do." Then she thought, *It may be the best policy, but it is not the easiest choice.*

Not wanting to go home right away, Honey

left her bike at the jewelry store and walked down Magic Row. She needed to think. By the time she reached Chillie Willies, she noticed a long, long line forming down the sidewalk.

"What is going on?"

As a young couple holding hands ran past her she heard the woman say, "Hurry, before they're all gone."

"All gone. Before what are all gone?"

13

Honey walked a few more paces and then decided to join the line. Joining lines in Sleepy Hollow was kind of hit or miss. You could be joining a line to something pretty amazing in a not-so-Halloweeny way or you could be joining a line that ended with you falling into a vat of pumpkin goo or getting the bejeebers scared out of you in a haunted house. Either way, it didn't matter to Honey today. Anything was better than going home with no locket. Anything was better than accusing her friends of being thieves.

The line was moving pretty quickly. Honey was trying to hear what some of the folks were saying because she had no clue where they were all going. She overheard one kid say something about Shivercicles. Shivercicles? She had never heard of such a thing before in Sleepy Hollow.

As the line continued to move, Honey tried to talk herself into telling her mother the truth. It was the right thing to do. But, on the other hand, there was no real hurry. Her phone jingled. This time it was Becky. Honey stared at her name for a few seconds and let the phone chime. Could it have been Becky? She *had* made a big deal about the locket, and she never got around to trying it on. And she did disappear for a long time during Harry's trick. Oh no! Honey shoved her phone into her coat pocket. As much as she hated to admit it, Becky, her best friend, was now the prime suspect in the case of the missing locket.

Honey felt just terrible about it. *Would Becky really steal from me?* Ugh. Honey walked a little farther, and the line stopped again just as she reached the Sleepy Hollow Magic Shoppe. Harry

Moon's favorite store. Harry went to the magic store pretty often, not only for magic supplies but to talk to the owner, Samson Dupree. He was an eccentric man who wore a gold crown and a purple cape. Samson was always giving Harry advice about how to deal with Mayor Kligore and life in general. Samson was a bit unusual. No one knew for certain how old he was or where he came from. But that was all right. It was part of what made him so interesting.

Honey thought about Harry's magic from time to time. Sometimes, she wished she had some magic of her own. Especially on a day like today. If only she had a magic wand she could wave to make the necklace reappear in her mom's jewelry box.

"I could talk to Samson," Honey whispered to herself. "Maybe he could help me."

Honey stared at the Magic Shoppe with its pretty yellow-and-red-striped awning. It wasn't like the other stores in Sleepy Hollow. Nothing Halloween about it. But no, Honey decided not to go inside. She gave a little wave to Samson as she passed by the shop's window. Samson Dupree was Harry's friend. She'd have to work this one out alone.

The line continued to move. Her phone jingled again. It was Becky—again. This time Honey answered.

"Hello," she mumbled.

"I thought we could go to the park," Becky said. "I have nothing going on today. I thought I might clean out my closet later and get rid of some of my kid stuff."

Honey sighed. "No, not today. I don't feel so great. Upset stomach. Mom says I should stay home."

"Oh, gee," Becky sounded disappointed. "But okay, I hope you feel better."

Honey ended the call and slipped the phone

back into her pocket. Another lie. How many lies had she told already? It was getting hard to keep track.

The line kept moving and with each step she took, Honey felt like she was being dragged further and further into a dark pit of lies and betrayal.

I'VE BEEN EXPECTING YOU

Finally, Honey Moon was only a few paces away from what everyone was so excited about. All she could do was stand there with her mouth open. She was looking at something that seemed impossible. It was a new shop at the end of Magic Row.

"Where did this come from? I've never seen

it before."

Honey looked around at all the people, but no one else seemed to be questioning the fact that a brand-new store had popped up on Magic Row. And pop up it did. Over night. From what Honey could tell, the people in line and the people going in and out of the store were acting like the shop had been there as long as all the others or they just didn't care that it didn't even exist yesterday.

But Honey was certain. She had driven right past this corner with her mom just the day before. And, even stranger, it was a brand-new building attached to the pet shop. "Come on," Honey said out loud. "How is this possible? This building didn't even exist yesterday."

"They make the best frozen bars in the world," she heard someone in line say. "And they're healthy too."

Honey looked around. Was she going crazy? Well, she knew her mom would be excited. "Mom'll love this place. They probably sneak kale or broccoli into every frozen pop."

Honey walked closer, and then she saw the name on the store window. SHIVER.

"Shiver?" Honey whispered. "Well, it certainly sounds like a store that belongs in Sleepy Hollow."

The store had a pretty ice-blue awning that hung over the wide front window. On

81

the window, in large letters, it read SHIVER. There was a skeleton head beneath the wording. And under that, it read, "You don't have to be bad to feel good." A bright blue carpet, about three feet wide, ran from the door to the curb and was very welcoming.

By now, Honey was standing on the carpet. It was her turn to enter the store as others poured out with ice pops in their hands. They all seemed thrilled. They looked like ice pops but they were not. She heard remarks like, "This is the best pomegranate frozen fruit bar I've ever eaten."

Pomegranate? she thought. Who makes pomegranate ice pops?

Honey pulled open the shop door, and that was when things got really weird. The crowd was gone, just gone. She was the only person in the store except for a woman standing behind the counter.

She was tall, young, and, Honey thought, very beautiful with long purple hair. Her lips were painted ruby. She wore a sky-blue apron with the same name, SHIVER, on the front and a scarf with Shivercicles all over it.

"Hello, Honey Moon," the woman said as she wiped her hands on her apron. "Welcome to Shiver."

Honey felt her eyebrows rise and her eyes grow big. "H-h-how do you know my name? Who are you? What is this place? Where did it come from? You weren't here yesterday."

Shiver grinned and shrugged. "Shivercicles. Who doesn't love a homemade Shivercicle? I've been expecting you," the woman said. "My name is Florence. But I prefer to be called by my last name—Shiver."

Honey raised her arm and wiggled-waved with just her fingers. "N-n-nice to meet you. But—"

"Don't worry," Shiver said. "Everything's cool. Pun intended."

Honey swallowed and stepped closer to the counter. "Shiver is a strange name."

Shiver laughed. "Hah. I wouldn't be too quick to say that, not with a name like Honey Moon."

"I guess," Honey said. "But I still don't get it. This store does not exist. And how do you know me?"

"Of course it does. You're standing in it. I see you got the backpack."

Turtle suddenly felt a little heavier on her back.

"What? My backpack?"

"Yeah, your mom gave it to you for Christmas. Sorry, it's not the most stylish thing in the world."

"Oh, Turtle has a certain style," Honey said with a smile. "But . . . but how—" Honey was feeling a little uneasy. It seemed Shiver knew a little too much about her.

"Oh, don't worry. Let's just say I put him in a place I was sure your mom would find him. When the time was right."

Honey looked around. *This is too weird,* she thought. She walked around and touched the chairs and the tall bistro tables. She even touched the counter and the cash register. It was an old-fashioned type with big keys and a big brass crank on the side. Not at all what you'd expect in a brand-new store.

"Seems real," Honey said. "But did you know your plant is dying?" Honey nodded toward a shriveled plant on the counter. It was in a purple container. The plant still had some green velvety leaves, but it seemed all the blooms were brown.

"Hmm, so it is."

Shiver laughed and walked out from behind the counter. She was wearing a long purple skirt with Shivercicles all over it under her apron. A strange pendant hung from her neck—it had a moon face but very different from the locket. It

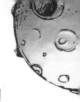

looked to be carved from a stone. Honey wanted to mention it but thought better of asking when Shiver walked to the shop window, hung the closed sign, and locked the door.

Honey swallowed and backed up. "Hey, why'd you do that? Let me out."

Instead of unlocking the door, Shiver turned toward Honey and smiled. "Let's you and me talk."

OLD FRIENDS, NEW FRIENDS

Honey was not scared at all—although even if she was feeling a bit frightened, it wouldn't be unusual. Sleepy Hollow was full of frights, and feeling scared was a pretty common state of mind. But the longer she stayed in the shop, the more peaceful she became.

"So," Shiver said, "not much luck at the

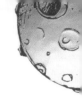

jewelry store, huh?"

Honey gasped. She crammed her hand into her pocket and felt for the pictures. They were still there. Phew. Then she put her hands on her hips and said, "Okay, you better tell me what is going on. Right now. Who are you, and how did you know about the jewelry store?"

Shiver fussed with a paper napkin. "He was right. Samson told me you were, shall we say, a spirited young woman."

"Samson? You know Samson Dupree?"

"Yep. We go way back. Way, way, wayyyyyy back. I even knew Astronomer Moon."

Honey clutched the pictures again. "He died in the 1800s! You couldn't have known him!"

Shiver's eyes twinkled with teeny, tiny stars. Her eyes were like a clear night sky. "Well, you know how Samson and, probably, your brother are always talking about there being a time for everything?"

Honey nodded. "Yes, but that's Harry stuff. That's what Samson says when it's time for Harry to wrangle with Mayor Kligore. I think he calls it the fullness of time."

"That's right," Shiver said. "Let's just say the time is full—full for you now."

"Me? I don't know what you mean. I'm not a

magician. What do you want from me?"

"For starters, you can tell me about the necklace."

Honey joined Shiver at the table. "Well, I just met you, and I don't really want to tell you. But I kind of think you know already."

Shiver didn't say anything. She only smiled.

"Here goes," Honey said. She told Shiver how she borrowed the necklace and about the sleepover, and then, with tears threatening, Honey said, "I'm mostly afraid Becky Young, my best friend *ever*, stole it. Or maybe it was Claire or Isabela, although I suspect her the least."

"I see," Shiver said.

"Did she?" Honey asked. "Did Becky take it, Shiver? Do you know where it is?"

Shiver stood and walked behind the counter. "Would you like a Shivercicle?"

"Yes. But what does that have to do with

the necklace?"

"Nothing," Shiver said.

Just then, a blueberry Shivercicle appeared in Honey's hand.

"You like blueberry, correct?"

"Hey! How did you do that?"

"Just enjoy it."

91

Honey bit the icy confection. It was the most delicious frozen bar imaginable. It tasted like real blueberry and made her feel warm inside, like she was playing in the park. "Wow. All those people are right. This is the best frozen treat I've ever eaten. First time I have ever eaten an ice pop that made me feel warm."

Shiver smiled. "My own recipe. Been making them for eons. King Arthur preferred strawberry, and Emily Dickinson had a thing for the ginger pops. Your ancestor Astronomer Moon liked banana buckwheat. Weird, but he liked them."

"Seriously?" Honey said. "Not about the banana buckwheat. I mean about all those people. You knew them? How is that possible? You don't look old."

"Sure did. I was friends with them all. And now, Honey Moon, I am your friend."

Honey reached into her pocket and felt for the pictures again. She had so many questions. "Maybe as my friend you can tell me if I'm right. Did Becky take it?"

Shiver's eyes twinkled. "Sorry, Honey Moon, it wouldn't be best for me to tell you everything. You will have to figure this one out on your own. Truth has a way of coming out, though. If it's the truth you are looking for, the truth is what you will find."

Honey touched one of the velvety petals on the counter plant. "Well, I think you need to face the truth about this plant."

Shiver smiled and nodded. "Righty right. Better do something about that. May I?" She indicated to Honey that she wanted her

Shivercicle.

"Sure."

Shiver leaned across the counter and let a few blue drops from the Shivercicle drip onto the leaves of the plant.

Right before Honey's eyes, the plant bloomed with delicate pink flowers.

Honey gasped. "How'd you do that?"

93

Shiver shook her head. "Oh, let's just say things aren't always what they appear to be. Never be surprised by what you will find when you come into Shiver."

Honey Moon touched one of the blooms. "This is beautiful. Violets, right?"

"Yep," Shiver said. "My favorites."

"So, you're a magician? Like Samson? Like Harry? Is that how you brought the flower back to life?"

Shiver laughed. "Not exactly. But kind of. I call it glimmering."

"Glimmering?" Honey wrinkled her nose. "What's that?"

Shiver lightly touched one of the velvety petals of the violet plant. "It starts when I get a notion or an idea. I have a glimmer or a twinkle or a flicker of what could be or should be and then a shiver—sometimes big, sometimes small, and then—" Shiver shrugged and wiggled her fingers in the air with a slight smile. "Poof."

"Poof?" Honey smiled widely. She had only heard the word *poof* used when Harry worked his magic. She never ever thought it could apply to anyone else in Sleepy Hollow.

"Poof," Shiver said. "What I see in my mind becomes real. It's something I would love to teach you."

Honey stepped back as her own shiver wriggled down her spine and right into her sneakers. "Me?"

94

"That's why I've come to Sleepy Hollow. To help you with your gift. You do have the gift, Honey Moon."

"Are you like Samson?"

Shiver nodded.

Honey gasped a little. About a million thoughts and questions ran through her mind. "I do? I mean I will?"

"Over time, Honey Moon. Over time. It will come to you. A little at first so don't go thinking you can make plants bloom."

"Oh, I won't." Honey's knees were shaking so hard they knocked. But it was good. She wasn't frightened. She felt excited. Like a new, exciting door had just been opened.

"Will it . . . will it," Honey swallowed. She wanted to ask the question that was burning a hole in her heart, but it was difficult. So, she pulled herself up and just blurted it out. "Will it help me find the necklace?"

95

Shiver's eyes twinkled with tiny fireworks. "No, that problem requires other means."

Shiver walked out from behind the counter. She stood close to Honey. "However, Honey, I am certain you will figure it out if you put your will to this." Shiver looked out the shop window. "Oh boy, the crowd is back. I better reopen."

Honey looked into the frozen Shivercicle case. "But there are no Shivercicles in there."

"There will be."

Honey took a deep, deep breath and shook her head. "I think it's going to be a lot of fun getting to know you, Shiver."

"Think about what you need to do. Think about what's best. Pay attention to the glimmers."

Shiver pulled open the door for Honey. "See you soon, Honey Moon. My door is always open for you."

The Fourteenth Store

Word of the Shiver Shoppe was everywhere by the time school started on Monday. Just about everyone in Sleepy Hollow had visited the store. In Honey's class, it was like Shiver madness had taken over.

"I had the strawberry," Noah said. "It was awesome."

"Me too," Jacob said. "I told my mom to buy a dozen."

Even Claire and Isabela were talking about the gourmet ice pops. But Honey sat at her desk quietly. She knew a little more about the shop and its owner than anyone in her class, maybe anyone in Sleepy Hollow. She also knew she couldn't really talk about her new friend. Who would believe that Shiver made a dead plant bloom or somehow made a hundred Shivercicles magically appear in an empty freezer in an instant?

More importantly, Honey enjoyed feeling like she and Shiver could be friends—she wanted to hold onto the good, new feeling forever. She had thought about telling Harry, but no, it was still so new.

And besides, she needed to find the locket. She needed to ask her friends. The problem was how to build up her courage to face them.

Mrs. Tenure clapped her hands, and the class quieted down. But even she was not immune to Shiver fever.

"My favorite was blackberry and the Sleepy Hollow Special," she said. "I went back three times this weekend." Then she smiled. "And the best part is they're good for you. Like the sign on the window reads: 'You don't have to be bad to feel good.'"

Hands shot up left and right as students wanted to share their Shiver experience. But Mrs. Tenure got the class back on track for the day and instructed the students to open their social studies books to page eighty-nine.

But Honey had a difficult time concentrating. She found herself staring through the windows and thinking about how Shiver had made the plant bloom. She also thought about why Shiver singled her out. Of all the people in Sleepy Hollow, Shiver had come to town to become Honey's friend. And she also couldn't help but think about the missing locket. She wondered how she could get Becky to confess to the crime—if Becky was really the thief. Honey cringed. She hated thinking about the possibilities.

At lunch that day, Honey sat with her usual group—Becky, Isabela, and Claire. She opened her paper sack. Her mom had packed tuna salad, carrots, and one oatmeal cookie. Honey purchased chocolate milk and a small bag of chips.

"So, Becky," Honey said. "You never got a chance to try on the necklace. Wanna come to my house after school today and try it on?"

Becky just shrugged. "No, I can't today."

"Awww, that necklace is all right," Claire said. "But I like the rubber ones with the words on them. You know, words like Be Brave."

"Yeah, yeah," Isabela said. "I like those too."

"But my locket is made from pure silver. It's valuable."

Becky shrugged again. "It's all right, Honey," she said. "Maybe another time. I've kind of . . . kind of lost interest."

Honey's heart sped. She didn't want to

believe that Becky had taken the locket. The thought made her very sad, but she had a glimmer that she should just let it go for now. So, she pushed the thought away. She picked at her sandwich and pulled the crust off. "I keep telling my mother to cut the crusts off."

"Me too," Claire said. "But she just laughs at me."

Honey noticed Isabel's sandwich. No crusts.

Isabela smiled. "Sorry, but Grace doesn't mind cutting the crusts."

"Give her time," Honey said.

✧

After school, Isabela and Becky invited Honey to play. Claire had basketball practice and dashed down the hall to the gym.

Honey looked into Becky's eyes. "No, not today. I have chores to do."

"Okay," Becky said. "I guess it's just Isabela

and me."

"Good," Honey said. "Have fun. Call me later."
But inside Honey was feeling pretty upset. She
just wanted Becky to tell the truth.

Honey dashed off and headed straight to
Magic Row.

She was on her way to Shiver, and just as
she reached the shop, she saw Mayor Kligore
standing outside the store. He was with Cherry
and Oink, his hound henchman. Cherry was
holding a long rolled up paper. Honey decided
to hang back for a minute and see what they
were doing because, even from where she was
standing, she could tell that Mayor Kligore was
awfully angry.

"It's unbelievable!" Mayor Kligore hollered.
"This shop should not be here!"

He grabbed the blueprints from Cherry.
"Look at this! Right here!"

He slapped the paper on Oink's back and
poked his finger onto a particular spot on the

page. Honey tried to see, but she couldn't really make out where exactly the mayor was pointing.

"Do you see a fourteenth shop in this row? DO YOU?"

Cherry shook her head.

"Of course, you don't! That's because there are only thirteen. There have ever only been thirteen shops! Thirteen shops in a row. That's the rule! *SO WHERE DID THIS SHIVER SHOPPE*

COME FROM!"

"I don't know, Boss Man. How do you explain it?" Cherry asked.

"Diabolical magic!" Mayor Kligore hollered. "It can only be magic! And not my kind. This is that confounding Samson Dupree's Deep Magic!"

Deep Magic? Honey had heard Harry talk about that. It was kind of the opposite of Mayor Kligore's dark magic.

Honey had moved a few steps closer when Shiver walked out of the shop. Honey stopped and smiled widely. Shiver would know how to deal with the mean old mayor.

"Hello, my name is Shiver." She held out a glistening red Shivercicle. "You must be Mayor Maximus Kligore. I've heard so much about you."

Mayor Kligore took a deep breath and started his familiar shaking from head to toe that everyone had become accustomed to when he got angry. Honey watched his face turn red with rage. "Just where did you and this Shiver Shoppe nonsense come from, miss whatever-your-name-is?" he screamed. "This store does not exist! It is not in the city plans, and even worse—" he paused to catch his breath, "even worse, *IT'S GOT NOTHING TO DO WITH HALLOWEEN!*"

Shiver shrugged. "Mmm. That is peculiar. But yet, here I am." She made a sweeping wave toward the store. "As you can see, me and my Shivercicles do exist."

Mayor Kligore shook the blueprint at Shiver. "There isn't even a sewer tie-in for this building. How did you get past my planning office? Where is your permit to run this . . . this frozen calamity?"

"Yeah," Oink said. "Frozen calamity contiguously connected to—"

"Silence, Hound," Kligore shouted. "Just shut up!"

That was when Shiver nodded toward Honey.

Honey moved closer so she could see the blue-print. Mayor Kligore never even noticed her. He was too upset to notice anything but Shiver and his own tirade.

"Oh dear," Shiver said. "Are you quite certain, Mayor, that my shop isn't in your plans? Perhaps you missed it. Look again."

This time the mayor marched toward his big black car. Cherry and Oink followed him. Shiver stepped closer, and Honey got as near as she could to see the blueprint when the mayor unrolled the paper on the hood of the car.

"See!" He frowned and tapped his finger on the blueprint. "Wait a minute. What's going on here? It's impossible."

"But isn't that the fourteenth store, Boss Man?" Cherry asked. She counted. "Yep. Fourteen. There is Shiver right there. Fourteen. Didn't notice it before."

Kligore crumpled the paper and shoved it into Cherry's hands. "Nothing happens in this town without my knowledge," he bellowed as he turned toward Shiver. Then he walked right up to her. The mayor and Shiver were nose to nose. "Nothing happens in this town without my permission," he growled. "Nothing. I don't know what games you and that Samson character are playing with my town, but you won't get away with it. That store wasn't here two days ago. I will get to the bottom of this. If you know what's good for you, you better be long gone before I do." He shivered. "I bet that Moon kid is messed up with this too."

Shiver shrugged. "Well, it's as clear as the warts on your hound's face. I'm here, and I'm here to stay."

Kligore backed away. "You haven't heard the last from me. You don't belong in *my* town."

Honey stepped closer to Shiver. Shiver took her hand and squeezed.

"Oh, that's just dandy," the mayor said. "You have a Moon child on your side. Well, we'll just see about that too."

Honey swallowed. Her knees shook, but she

held onto Shiver and forced a smile at the mayor. "That's right, Mayor Kligore. Shiver is my friend."

"Well, Honey Moon," Kligore said, "you've fallen into bad company. Very bad company, indeed."

"I go where I'm needed," Honey said.

Shiver raised her hand and waved with just her fingers. "Bye-bye." Then she whispered to Honey. "Funny how he resorts to name-calling and insults when he doesn't understand."

Kligore and his employees piled into the car like clowns, one on top of the other. The mayor shook his fist out the window. "I'll be back!"

"He does go on about things, doesn't he?" Shiver said as the black Phantom Lustro squealed away from the curb.

"He sure does," Honey said. "That's our lovable mayor. And it doesn't look like he is thrilled about your Shivercicles."

CONFRONTATION

Honey followed Shiver into the Shiver Shoppe.

But, before she could say anything, Samson Dupree walked out from behind the counter.

"Bravo," he said. "I'm so glad I put my "Back In A Flash!" sign in the magic shop window and came to visit. That was fun to watch."

Honey sneezed.

"Oh," Honey said. "Mr. Dupree, I didn't know you were here. How are you?"

"I'm fine, Honey Moon," Samson said. "But I suppose you are not very fine."

Honey looked at Shiver. "Did you tell him?"

"I didn't need to," Shiver said.

Honey took a breath and sat at one of the tables. "I don't know if I'll ever get used to this town."

"It's all right, Honey," Shiver said. "Samson and I are old friends."

"Very, very old," Samson said. "I've known Shiver and her family forever it seems. Just like I've known your family over the years, including Astronomer Moon."

Honey felt her eyebrows rise. "You . . . you knew Astronomer Moon?"

Samson stepped closer to Honey, "Fascinating man. Important man."

"I know," Honey said. "My dad told me some amazing things about him. He told us he was a traveler and an archaeologist."

"That's correct," Shiver said. "A very good one."

Honey nodded. "And now I've lost him."

"That's what I understand," Samson said.

"But . . . but I'm pretty sure I know who has him, I mean it—the necklace, the locket. It might be Becky Young, but I just don't want to believe that. Or maybe Claire. Or maybe even Isabela is playing some trick. She likes practical jokes. Yeah, maybe that's it—someone who likes to play tricks."

Samson laughed. "I heard about the syrup. Very sweet trick to pull on Harry."

Honey shook her head. "Did Harry tell you?"

"Of course," Samson said. "I think his hair is still sticky."

Honey jumped off the bistro stool. "I've been thinking about those strawberry Shivercicles all day. May I have one, please?"

112

"You certainly may," Shiver said.

Shiver handed Honey a red Shivercicle. "Now, these Shivercicles here are my specials. The strawberry one is one of my favorites. Very calming."

"Thank you," Honey said, taking a slurp and feeling almost instantly soothed. "But I'd rather you tell me who took it. Who stole the locket?"

Shiver looked toward the violet plant. The pretty pink blooms were shriveling away.

113

"Why did that happen?" Honey asked.

"It's quite a sensitive plant. Honey. After all, didn't you take the necklace first—without permission?"

Honey bit into her Shivercicle. It was so cold. "But I was planning to put it right back. I just wanted to try it for a little while. I only borrowed it."

"And now look what happened," Shiver said.

Honey swallowed.

"You know," Samson Dupree said with a big smile, "I remember a time when Harry did something similar. He ended up telling lies to pretty much everyone who crossed his path until he finally confessed."

Honey remembered. It was the day Harry went to Boston on the train without permission to check out some famous magic store.

114

"Yeah, that was pretty serious. He got grounded."

"For a month," Samson said. "But he felt better after telling the truth."

"But even if I tell my mother, I still need to find the locket first."

"Uhmmmmm," Shiver said. "That's true. I suggest you put on your Sherlock Holmes hat and do some investigating."

"I will." Honey finished her Shivercicle just as a group of teenagers entered the store. Harry was among them.

"Hey," he said. "Hey, Samson. What are you doing here?"

Honey only nodded toward him. "I have to go."

"Wait up a second," Harry called. "Did you find the—"

But Honey managed to get outside the shop before Harry could finish his question. She knew what he was talking about. She froze for a second near the curb. "I have to hurry and solve this crime before Harry tells on me."

Honey took off down the street. She ran as hard as her legs could carry her. She didn't know if she was running *from* something or *toward* something. She only knew she wanted to get as far away from the problem as she could. But, when she reached the park, she knew. There was no place far enough away that she could hide from the truth.

With her head low, Honey walked on. For

the first time since this whole thing started, she felt guilty. Here she had been blaming her best friends when she was the one who took the necklace in the first place. Two crimes had been committed, and Honey thought she would do just about anything to turn back time. If only Shiver's magic could do that.

"Honey! Over here!"

Honey looked up and saw Claire. She and Isabela were playing catch. Claire had just thrown a high fly, which Isabela managed to catch with a leaping dive.

"Honey!"

She looked around, and she saw Becky sitting under a tree. She had a book in her hands.

"Hi," Honey called. But at the same time her stomach sunk into her sneakers. She needed to confront her best friend. Was this the time?

Honey walked slowly to Becky. "I thought Claire had basketball practice."

"She did, but it was cancelled. Coach Varsity wasn't in school today."

"Oh, okay." Honey sat down next to Becky. She pulled her knees up to her chest. Her heart pounded like a drum. She wanted to find just the right words.

"So, what's up?" Becky said. "I thought you had chores."

"I-I did them," Honey lied.

117

"Oh, cool," Becky said. "Are you okay? You seem weird."

"Yeah," Honey said. "It's just that I need to ask you—"

Before Honey could get the words out, Becky jumped up. "Oh no, I have to go. I forgot. My-my mother needs me."

"Wait," Honey called. "Did you take—"

Becky was gone, and Honey was both relieved and sad. Did Becky run off because she

knew the question Honey was about to ask?

"What?" Claire asked. "I just came over to see if you wanted to toss the ball around, and I heard what you said to Becky. You think she took your stupid old necklace?"

"I-I don't know," Honey said. Tears welled in her eyes. This was getting out of hand. "Maybe."

118

Honey could not fight back her emotions. This was the most terrible ache she had ever felt. And it was all her fault. If only she had never borrowed the locket.

"How could you think that about Becky? She's the most honest person I know. Do you suspect me too? Or Isabela? We were all at your house that night."

Honey stood. "I said I don't know."

"Well, I didn't steal it," Claire said. "I thought you were my friend."

That was when Isabela raced over. "What's

going on?"

"Honey thinks one of us stole her necklace," Claire said.

Isabela gasped. She looked away and down the road like she was thinking. "Maybe Harry is playing a magic trick."

Honey shook her head. "No. I asked him."

"And you believe him," Claire said, "but not us."

Isabela's phone chimed. "Oh, gee, time's up. I have to go home. I'm supposed to walk Bart. See you *mañana*." Isabela ran off.

"I have to go too," Claire said. "See ya, Sherlock. Good luck with the case. You can cross these two friends off your suspect list."

Honey watched the girls run off. This was turning out to be her worst day ever.

She walked on toward home. When she reached the street, a car slowed down. It was

her mother.

"Hey, Mom," Honey said when Mary Moon lowered the window.

"Want a ride home?" Mary asked.

"No, I'd rather walk."

Mary Moon smiled. "Okay, sweetheart. See you at home."

Honey watched her mother drive off. Now, it seemed all the people she cared about most in the world were gone. She was left standing on the curb—alone, with no idea what to do next.

She saw her mother's car turn the corner onto Nightingale Lane. Honey sighed. "Sorry Mom. I know I need to tell you."

As Honey stepped into the street to cross, she felt a slight shiver down her spine.

That's weird, she thought.

GUILTY

oney took her time heading home. Dinner was already on the table by the time she got there.

"Oh, there you are, Honey," her mom said. "I was beginning to think you got lost even though I just saw you down the street." Then she smiled, which made the sick feeling in Honey's stomach a little bit worse.

"No," Honey said. "I just took my time."

Mary Moon set a large salad bowl practically overflowing with leafy greens and radishes on the table.

"Mom," Honey said. "I need to—"

Before she could get her whole sentence out, Harry burst into the kitchen.

122

"There you are," he glared at Honey. His hair was still sticking up from the syrup prank. "You know, I still can't get all the goo out of my hair. I've washed it a dozen times."

Honey couldn't help it. She laughed just a little when she saw him. She did try to apologize through the laughter. "I'm sorry. It was Isabela's idea."

"Oh, don't blame someone else. You are still guilty. *Ugh.*" Harry sat at his place at the table. "You still laughed."

Honey sat also, but she wasn't smiling

anymore. It seemed no matter who she talked to, she was reminded of what she did. She mostly suspected Becky. But it was still possible it was Claire or even Isabela. She also knew that no matter who took it or where it might be now, this whole mess was originally her fault.

She watched Mary Moon snap a bib on Harvest. "Shivercicle," he said.

Mary Moon shook her head. "He's been asking for Shivercicles all day. Maybe we'll take him over to that new store."

Honey swallowed. "Good idea. They really are good." She was trying her best to at least seem happy.

John Moon walked into the kitchen carrying a copy of the town newspaper, which he folded and placed on the sideboard. "I was just reading about that new store," he said as he sat at the table. "The mayor is kind of upset about it."

"Yeah," Harry said. "Samson told me that Mayor Kligore didn't have any idea the store was opening."

"That's because it's magical," Honey said.

John laughed. "Magical? No, we already have one magic shop in Sleepy Hollow."

Mary Moon took her place next to Harry. "Let's get settled into our dinner. Then we can discuss magic or not magic."

124

"Good idea, Mary," John said.

Mary Moon put some salad on Harvest's plate and passed the bowl around the table. Little Harvest picked up a radish and licked it. "Shivercicle."

"Shivercicles?" John said. "What's so special about those things, anyway?"

"They're really good, Dad," Harry said. "Lots of odd flavors."

"And they are a much better choice over traditional frozen bars," Mary said. "More healthy. I understand they're made from real fruits and veggies. Less sugar."

"Veggies? In popsicles?" John pretended to gag. "I don't know about that."

Honey was quiet. She was kind of glad no one asked her to explain what she meant about the store being magical, even after she had said it. She was even more glad her mother seemed to forget that Honey was just about to tell her something before Harry stormed in with his sticky hair situation.

Honey pushed spaghetti around her plate. She really wasn't very hungry. The lump in her stomach had inflated to the size of a basketball.

"What's the matter, Honey?" her mom asked. "You feeling all right?"

"Sure, Mom. I just finished a Shivercicle. Guess I'm full."

"I keep telling you no snacks so close to

dinner."

"Sorry, Mom," Honey said.

Harry slurped some spaghetti strands into his mouth and made Harvest laugh. "But it is still really weird," he said. "The mayor knows everything that goes on in town. How come he didn't know about Shiver?"

"Because Shiver didn't want him to know," Honey said.

"Shiver," John said. "That's a weird name for a person."

"She is a bit strange. I met her," Harry said.

"No more weird than Samson Dupree," Honey said. "I like her. I think she's the neatest person in Sleepy Hollow."

"Okay, okay, settle down," John said. "Harry's entitled to his opinion and so are you."

Honey looked at her mother. "May I be

excused. I–I have a lot of homework."

"Yes," Mary Moon said.

"Hold on," John Moon said. "Honey, you need to eat something."

"It's all right," Mary said. She put her hand on John's arm. "We all need a little space sometimes, and if she has homework—"

"I do," Honey said. She pushed her chair under the table.

"Don't forget, Honey," Mary Moon said, "you and Harry are babysitting Friday night."

"I know, Mom," Honey said.

Honey fell face down on her bed. It truly was the worst day ever. She had told so many fibs she couldn't keep track anymore, and she had been so close to telling her mother the truth but then didn't. The hole she had dug for herself was getting deeper and deeper. She sat straight up as the most terrible thought entered her mind.

"Friday night! What if Mom wants to wear the locket Friday night?"

The gloom and doom she had been feeling doubled and then tripled. She had to get the locket back. Time was of the essence. Honey hugged Turtle to her chest. "I know you don't really speak," she whispered, "but I could sure use your help."

Her phone chimed. It was Becky.

"Hi," Honey said.

"We have to work on that project," Becky said.

Honey was silent. She had completely forgotten about the big social studies project. "Oh yeah," she said into the phone.

"But, I don't feel well," Becky said. "I can't come over."

"Oh, that's all right," Honey said. "I don't feel good either. Goodbye."

Turtle's big googly eyes spun like the tea cups at Disney World.

Usually, she could talk to Becky for a long time about all sorts of things: schoolwork, music, clothes. But not tonight. She suspected that Becky wasn't really sick, sick. She was guilty sick like Honey.

129

Honey reached for the *Alice in Wonderland* book. She opened it—just in case the locket had magically reappeared. But no, the locket was still missing.

Honey lay on her bed trying to muster up her courage to do one of two things. She had to either tell her mother the truth or confront Becky.

She heard Harry in the hallway. She always knew when Harry was stomping down the hall.

And that made her think of a third possibility. She could ask Harry again to use his magic. Or find a way to use that glimmer thing that Shiver was talking about. But she wasn't really sure how to do that.

Honey dashed to Harry's room and burst inside without knocking.

"You again!" Harry exclaimed. "Didn't Dad tell you to stop coming in here without knocking?"

"Sorry," Honey said. "But this is an emergency."

"What kind of emergency?"

"Life and death," Honey replied.

She stood near Harry. Her knees were knocking. She was so nervous and a little scared.

"I still can't find the locket."

"I figured," Harry said. "But, I already told

you I can't help. My magic is no good with stealing."

"Yes, you can," Honey said. "When I was at Shiver today I saw Samson Dupree."

"Samson? I saw him too. Why was he there? Is he into Shivercicles?"

"Shiver and he are like really, really old friends. I told you she was magical."

Harry shook his head. "Just because Samson wanted a Shivercicle doesn't mean Shiver is magic."

"Well, she is," Honey said. "But so are you. Samson told me at the store that he knew I lost the locket, and that's making me think the locket might be magic too."

"No way," Harry said. "It's just a family heirloom."

132

"But Samson said he knew Astronomer Moon, which means maybe Astronomer Moon was a magician too. Like you. Maybe that's where you get it, you know?"

"My magic comes from the Great Magician." Harry grunted. "It's not hereditary."

Honey snorted air out of her nose. "But what if Astronomer was a magician and the locket was magic like your wand?"

"You are really stretching, kiddo." Harry said.

Honey sat on Harry's bed. "Please, Harry. Can you use your magic to make it reappear? Maybe it will hear you like your wand does. I've seen you call it, and it comes to you."

Harry sat at his desk. "I don't know, Honey. It sounds too crazy."

"Please, I'm desperate. I'll do all your chores for a month."

Harry picked up his wand. "I'll try, but I doubt this will work."

He stood and said, "Silver locket, silver locket. We know that you are missing. Please come back, please come back, and land in Honey's pocket. Abracadabra."

Honey jumped off the bed. She shoved her hands in her pockets, but then her heart sank. No locket.

"See," Harry said.

"You weren't really trying that time. Put more

feeling into it."

"Honey," Harry said. "This isn't just about finding the locket. It's about telling the truth, and for that, you'll need to find your own magic. I kind of think the locket will make its own way back to Mom then."

Honey sighed. "I guess I need to tell her."

"You really do," Harry said. "The sooner the better."

A TANGLED WEB

Honey didn't talk to her mother that night. She didn't talk to her the next morning either. She tried a couple of times, but mornings were always so busy. Honey just couldn't get the words out when her mother was alone. Or maybe, just maybe Honey didn't really *want* to tell her mother the truth. She even sneaked into her parent's bedroom and checked the jewelry box. Just in case it magically reappeared. But no. It was still missing, of course.

School was not much better. Claire and Isabela were barely speaking to Honey. All Claire would say was that she did not appreciate being a suspect and that she would never steal a dumb old locket. Honey tried to make it right. But she couldn't. They were all still angry.

At lunch, they still all sat at their usual table, but it was the quietest table in the whole cafeteria. Isabela said, "Do you still think one of us stole it?"

"I don't know anymore," Honey said. "I just know I can't find the locket—anywhere."

"Did you shake the book?" Isabela asked.

Honey looked at Isabela cross-eyed. "Of course I shook the book. I almost ripped the pages out. It was the first place I looked. And the last. I've checked the book a hundred times."

"Maybe it dropped behind your bed or your

bookshelf," Claire said. She sounded a little nicer. Maybe because Honey had to swipe some tears away.

Becky had no suggestions about where to look. She hurried her lunch and then said, "I have to go to the art room. I got permission to work on a project during recess."

As much as she hated the thought, Honey still suspected Becky the most because she kept running away. If only she could just get Becky to confess, then the whole thing would be over. Maybe. On the way back to class, Honey thought about what she would do if she discovered Becky took the locket. How could she ever trust her friend again?

The next few days were not much better. Honey tried to get things back to normal with her friends by not discussing the locket. The trouble was every time they were together her thoughts immediately turned back to Astronomer Moon and where on earth he could be hiding. She visited with Shiver again, but the big social studies project had taken up a lot of her time. Since it was a project with Becky, it was a little strange. So strange that Becky did most of her work at her house while Honey did her share at her house.

Becky had said it only made sense. "I have to do the drawing and coloring, and I really don't need you for that."

Honey agreed. "And I have the writing."

So, they worked separately. It was something that even Honey's mother thought was out of the ordinary.

"How come you and Becky aren't working together?" she asked at dinner. "Isn't the project due Friday? It's already Wednesday. Not much time left."

"Oh, we are," Honey said. Then she swallowed. Hard. Because she knew what she was about to say next was a total lie. "We are doing the work at school. Mrs. Tenure gives us time."

Mary Moon seemed satisfied with that answer, and Honey thought she was very clever for devising the lie—another new feeling.

By the time Thursday rolled around, Claire didn't seem quite as angry at Honey. She even suggested that maybe, just maybe, Honey was right for suspecting them.

"I might have jumped to the same conclusion," Claire said. "It still hurts though. And just so you know, Honey, I would never ever steal from you or anyone."

139

"Thanks," Honey said.

Still, the fact remained that the locket was missing, and whoever had it was not confessing.

After school on Friday, Honey didn't feel like hanging out with her friends. She just wanted some alone time. And one of her favorite places to think was the old Sleepy Hollow Cemetery. She enjoyed walking among the stones and sitting near one of her favorite authors—Louisa May Alcott, the author of *Little Women*. About half-way there, she heard someone calling her name. She turned and saw Becky.

"Becky? What's up?" Honey said. "I said I didn't feel like playing."

Becky stopped running. She huffed and puffed a little and then said, "Honey, I just want you to know that I still want to be your friend."

Honey felt her forehead wrinkle. Was Becky getting ready to confess? She should ask Becky right now—point blank—about the necklace. But she didn't. Instead, she said, "I want to be friends too, but I just need to be alone now."

"Oh, sorry," Becky said. "I'm really sorry. About everything." And then she ran off toward the park.

Honey stood outside the cemetery gate. Not too many people visited the place, at

least not on a school day, but today she saw someone walking around. She moved a little closer and recognized Mayor Kligore walking among the stones. She had never seen the mayor here before, but he was the mayor so maybe it wasn't too strange. For the first time, she didn't feel like running away from him. Mayor Kligore kind of scared Honey. He was always so loud and mean. He yelled a lot.

She pushed open the gate. Honey winced at the screeching sound it made that caused the mayor to look straight at her. Now she felt nervous. Now her heart pounded. He was walking toward her.

Honey's first instinct was to run, but for some reason, she didn't.

142

Mayor Kligore walked close to her. "Well, if it isn't the Moon girl. You seem a little down in the dumps, child." He looked around and waved his arm. "Perhaps a little grave. Ha ha ha."

Honey swallowed as Turtle became heavier and heavier. There was no way she wanted to let Mayor Kligore know he, or the cemetery, frightened her. Instead, she pulled herself up to her full height and said, "Yeah, it's me, Mayor Kligore. How's it going?"

Mayor Kligore laughed and then turned grim. "So, what's the trouble? That infernal brother of yours bugging you too?"

Honey said, "No. Of course not. He doesn't bother me. Not like he bothers you. I just lost something. Something special. It belongs to my mother."

"Ahhhhh, I see," Mayor Kligore said. "Did you lose it here in my playground?"

"No," Honey said. "I just come here when—"

"I know," Mayor Kligore interrupted. "It is a good thinking spot. Nothing clears the head better than a walk among the dear departed. They don't talk back."

Honey smiled at his silly joke.

"So tell me, Honey, how did you come to lose this special something?" Kligore rubbed his hands together and grinned. Well, kind of. It was more like a smirk—almost like he knew something already.

Honey told him. She wasn't sure why, but she blurted out the whole thing. The instant she was finished she regretted ever having come to

143

the cemetery.

"Please don't tell my mother," Honey begged. "I'll confess. I really will. Today. I promise."

Kligore looked at Honey thoughtfully. "No, no, of course not, my dear girl. Calm down. I happen to be on your side. I always say deception is the best policy. Don't you agree? You've done a grand job of . . . deception so far. Why not keep it up?"

144

"Keep up the lying?" Honey said. "But—"

"It's the easiest way to deal with your little predicament. It's just lovely how one little, tiny fib can mushroom into a giant bundle of lies."

Honey swallowed. "I'll say. I've told so many already. It's hard to keep track."

"But the human brain is a marvel," Mayor Kligore said. "Eventually you will start believing your own lies, and that's when it gets truly masterful. Bwahahaha." Kilgore stuck his hands deep into his pockets. "Trust me, it happens."

"Masterful?" Honey said. "But I don't want to be a master liar."

"Oh, don't fret, Moon girl. Once caught in the tangled web, it can be rather difficult to get out."

"Shiver says I should tell the truth."

The mayor's eyes grew wide. His face reddened. "Shiver. She's nothing. Don't listen to her. She'll be gone by morning. Count on it."

145

Honey did not like where this was going. Her whole body felt like it was on fire.

"I-I-I better be going," Honey said. "I'm late for supper."

Honey turned away from the mayor.

"Hey, Moon girl," he called after her. "I might be able to help you. I might be able to find that priceless family heirloom and uncover the thief."

"Really," Honey said. She stopped and turned

back around. "You? But how?"

"Hmm, come back here tomorrow, same time. I'll have the answers you are looking for. Of course, there may be a small charge for my services, but nothing you can't handle. Now, I must be going. I have business to attend."

Honey watched the mayor duck into his car. She didn't know what to say. It sounded good, but what exactly was the mayor going to do? How could he know who took the necklace? *He must be planning to use his dark magic,* Honey thought as she put her hand to her chest. Her heart pounded like mad. *Harry couldn't use his magic, but Kligore is going to offer his?* The web was getting tighter and tighter.

Dark Secrets and Deep Holes

oney wandered around the cemetery for a little while reading the grave stones and straightening up some fallen potted geraniums. At least it wasn't pouring rain. But mostly, she was wishing Becky would just tell the truth and admit she took the necklace. Mostly, she was wishing she could find

the courage to tell her mother the truth.

This all was feeling so strange to Honey. She had always been able to talk to her mother. After all, her mother loved her more than anyone ever could. And she had never ever lied to her mother about anything. Honey plucked a brown leaf from a maple tree. The tree and its leaves were trapped inside Halloween just like everything else in the town. She held the red-and-orange leaf in her palm and then crumpled it to dust. That was kind of how her heart felt, like it could just crumble.

But then an odd sensation covered her. A darker thought that she had not yet entertained came to her. It was as though a spell had taken root. Honey said, "Yeah. It's all Becky's fault. If she'd just tell the truth and give me back the necklace, I could put it back in my mother's jewelry box, and she'd never know I took it."

The very thought made her angry. It was like a voice was telling her that the real person she should be angry with was Becky. Honey was building up a full head of steam when she

marched out of the cemetery. She even balled her hands into tight fists. "I'm gonna tell her a thing or two. She got me into this mess." She felt so angry she didn't even feel Turtle on her back anymore.

Honey marched on toward Becky's house. Step after step, her anger grew until she saw Harry racing down the street on his bike. He stopped with a squeal of the tires.

"Hey, what gives? You look like you could chew through nails," he said.

"I could," Honey said. "I'm so mad at Becky for taking that necklace I could scream."

"Whoa, hold on a second. Cool your jets. She's not the only guilty party here. And you are not a hundred percent certain she took it."

Honey snorted air out her nose like a bull. "I am too. I can tell by the way she's been acting. Running away all the time. Making up excuses."

"So? Who ran away from the dinner table

K

ER

last night? And who's been telling one fib after another?"

Honey's fists grew tighter. "But it's her fault. If she'd just give it back, I could return it, and Mom would never know. I wouldn't have to lie like Mayor Kligore told me I should."

Harry dropped his bike on the grass. "Wait a second. Kligore? Have you been talking to the mayor? What does he have to do with this?"

5

Honey shook her head. "I just talked to him. In the cemetery. He told me lying is always the best thing to do. He said if I keep lying, it will get easier the more I do it. If I can't get the locket back, I'll just tell Mom I don't know what happened to it."

"Holy cow. Now, *I'm* angry," Harry said, stomping his foot. "Don't you get it? Mayor Kligore is just trying to get you to cross that line."

"Which line?"

"The line between the Deep Magic and his pitiful dark magic."

"Ohhhh," Honey said. "Did he put a spell on me?"

"Kind of. Let's just say he influenced you and made you believe a lie. See how it works?"

"Wow. I was just about to go holler at Becky."

Harry shook his head. "Find a better way, Honey. The truth is always the better policy. Always! Maybe you should visit Samson Dupree. He's a pretty smart dude."

151

"Nah, I have Shiver. She'll help me."

"Well, talk to someone just so you get it figured out. And soon. Mom's probably gonna want to wear that necklace tonight."

Harry rode off. Honey noticed that Harry's magic wand was sticking out of his back pocket. "I wish I had a magic wand that would make all of this go away."

It was difficult to pull out of Mayor Kligore's spell because he had such a powerful effect on the people of Sleepy Hollow, but Honey turned around and headed for Magic Row. *I have to find Shiver. Right now.*

As she approached the row of shops in town, she saw that Mayor Kligore and his carful of creeps were now at Shiver. The mayor was standing outside ranting about something again. Honey moved closer and hid behind a lamppost. It might not be right to listen in on conversations, but this sounded important.

"And furthermore, Miss Shiver," Kligore bellowed, "I keep having that same dang blasted nightmare, night after night."

Honey could see Shiver's bright smile from where she was standing. Shiver was always so calm and collected. She stood near Kligore, tall and in charge. "Nightmare?" she said noticing Honey with a tiny nod. "What nightmare is that?"

"Don't give me that," Kligore hollered. " You know exactly the one. The one with the-the

Shivercicles. Hundreds of them, no thousands, no a legion. A legion of-of your ginormous Shivercicles chasing me all over Folly Farm. It's a frozen army of icy monsters trying to freeze me."

"Oh, dear," Shiver said. "I can see how an army of Shivercicles could be scary. That must be awful. How do you sleep?"

"Scary is not the word. AND I'M NOT SLEEPING!

153

It's annoying, and it's all your fault. Now get out of my town. Or I'll—"

"You'll what?" Shiver asked. She took a step closer. "You'll what, Mr. Mayor? Melt my Shivercicles? I'll just make more." Shiver stood toe to toe with Kligore. "You have had your way with this town long enough. It's time to let these people have their lives back."

Honey snickered. She liked the idea of Shivercicles chasing the mayor around the farm.

Kligore backed away. His eyes blazed with fury. *"NEVER!"* That was when Oink hopped out of the Phantom Lustro and approached his boss. Honey couldn't hear what Oink whispered to the mayor. But, the mayor did seem to calm down, although his hands were still balled into tight fists. That made Honey remember how she had gotten so angry at Becky just a few minutes ago. It reminded her of how one rotten apple can infect the whole barrel and how Mayor Kligore had a way of getting people to think just like him.

"Now look here," the mayor said, taking a deep breath and making a very bad attempt at lowering his voice. "I don't care how you do it but just disappear. Go out the same way you came in. Use whatever . . . magic you might have at your disposal and leave Sleepy Hollow."

Honey crept a little closer. She felt safe knowing that Shiver saw her. And besides, Kligore was so blinded by his anger that she doubted he noticed her.

155

"I'm afraid not, Mr. Kligore," Shiver said, straightening her skirt. "I'm not going anywhere. Not yet anyway. I have work to do here in Sleepy Hollow, and I intend to finish my business."

Kligore was starting to fume again. Honey was pretty sure she could see steam coming from his ears.

"It's too bad," Shiver said. "If you weren't so enamored by your own personality and thirst for fame and fortune, you might have noticed that your little Halloween spell is," she took a step closer and was just about nose-to-nose with the mayor, "starting to crack!"

Kligore took another step back. "Crack? That's nonsense. How? Why? When?" Then he fell silent and just stood there like a big, dumb statue. Honey half expected to see a few ravens land on his shoulders.

Shiver shook her head. "Tsk, tsk, tsk. Brain freeze? Is that what's happening? Maybe a spicy pumpkin Shivercicle will warm you."

156

Kligore seemed to wake up. "NO! I detest pumpkin spice."

"Now that is odd coming from a man who is all about Halloween."

Honey moved even closer. By now, she was standing near the shop window.

"I see you trying to hide, Honey Moon," Mayor Kligore said. "I know you are in cahoots with this–this frozen Shivercicle woman. I suggest you get home now while you still can."

Honey was just about to say something when Shiver turned and put her finger to her lips. "Shhhhh. Just wait."

Honey smiled. "Go, Shiver."

"You have no idea who I am, Kligore. I am so much more than your silly dream. As you've no doubt figured out by now. I am your worst nightmare. Well, me and my Shivercicles."

Honey giggled. "Looks like there will be more Shivercicles chasing him tonight."

157

"No, no," Kligore said. "I was just at the town hall. You don't even have the proper permits to legally open this business."

Honey thought, *Ugh, even he must know that's a lame thing to say now. Shiver could get that paperwork done with a simple nod.*

Shiver snapped her fingers. "Done and done."

"Way to glimmer, Shiver," Honey whispered.

The mayor let out a huge snort. "Then maybe Honey Moon will be interested in what I have to say."

Honey's heart sped.

"I told you to meet me at the cemetery tomorrow, remember?"

Honey nodded.

158

"Well, I will just tell you now. I had my hounds do a little snooping on the big screen."

"Big screen?" Honey said.

Shiver smiled into Honey's eyes. "Just a toy he uses to spy on Sleepy Hollow. Nothing to worry about. It's how he keeps tabs on Harry."

"Stop telling my secrets, you awful creature," Kligore said.

"Secrets, Kligore." Shiver said. "Tsk, tsk. Secrets can be so dark unless you're keeping a secret about a surprise birthday party."

Honey smiled. But then she felt sad. She herself was hanging on to a dark secret.

"A secret," Shiver said, "especially a wicked one, has a way of getting heavier and heavier the longer you carry it, until finally—"

"Enough of your jibber jabber, you frozen old magpie." Kligore interrupted her.

Honey felt frozen herself. She moved back toward the store.

159

Kligore looked straight at her. "The person who took your precious necklace is—"

But then, suddenly, Kligore's jaw clamped down. He couldn't speak. All he could do was mumble with closed lips. "Mummblembun." He shook his head violently trying to speak. "Mummblebum. Mugwhomps. Mumble."

"Ahh, I like him much better this way," Shiver said.

Kligore turned away mumbling and clawing

at his lips and marched toward the Lustro. Oink followed him without saying a word.

"But he was going to tell me," Honey said. "Why wouldn't you let him tell me for sure. I mean I think I know but—"

"It was not his news to tell," Shiver said. "All in good time. As one of the Great Magician's wisest friend once said, 'Whatever was is. Whatever will be, is. That's how it always is with the Great Magician."

Honey followed Shiver into the shop. She thought she understood what Shiver was trying to tell her.

"You know all about the Great Magician too?" Honey said.

"Certainly," Shiver said. "I know him well."

Honey climbed up on one of the chairs. She looked around the bright shop. Shiver had hung posters of encouraging words and Shivercicles and none of them seemed to help. "I almost let myself get influenced by Mayor Kligore."

"How? What do you mean?" Shiver asked.

"At the cemetery. He told me to keep lying, and then it was like a weird power came over me. I was, all of a sudden, even more angry with Becky. So angry that I was gonna march right over and—"

"And then Harry stopped you."

"Yes, I'm glad he did. How did you know that?"

"Is that a surprise? And yes, I am glad he stopped you," Shiver said. "So what do think? Is it finally time to make this right?"

"Can I have a pineapple pop first?"

"Sure," Shiver said." My pineapple pop will give you confidence to do the right thing. One of my specialties. You sit there, enjoy a Shivercicle, and figure out the right words. You have them." She pointed to her heart. "Right

161

inside."

Honey thought and thought, but the words were not coming to her. "Shiver," she said, "I think I should just let the words happen when I need them."

"Yes, what is it the Great Magician says? He will give you the right words in all good time."

"Yep," Honey said. "But Shiver, I still feel angry at Becky . . . well, Becky and myself."

"I suggest you head over to the park," Shiver said. "It's time to face the music as they say."

"I'm not a fan of this music," Honey said.

LOST AND FOUND

oney headed toward the park. She needed to hurry. It was getting near dinner time, the sun was setting, and a chilly breeze had started to blow. Leaves swirled at her feet, and squirrels hurried about collecting the acorns falling from the trees.

"I wonder why Shiver sent me to the park?" she said as she walked. Turtle had grown just a bit heavier now.

She saw Becky sitting on one of the park benches. "Ah, that's why."

Becky was huddled in a heavy blue coat. She wore a yellow knit cap pulled over her ears.

"Hi," Honey said as she approached Becky.

Becky didn't say anything right away. She only looked at Honey. Honey saw tears in Becky's eyes.

164

"I'm glad I found you," Honey said.

"Me too. I was hoping you'd find me." Becky wiped tears away. "I'm sorry, Honey. I took the necklace." Becky broke into tears.

"I knew it," Honey said. "I just knew it. I thought maybe Claire or Isabela might have taken it. But I was more worried it was you. How could you? You're supposed to be my best friend."

Becky reached into her coat pocket. She pulled out the necklace. Honey snatched it away. "I could get into so much trouble because of this. I never want to speak to you again!"

"But Honey, I–I said I was sorry."

"Sometimes, sorry isn't enough." Honey ran off toward home with the necklace securely in her hand. With each footfall, she switched back and forth between being angry at Becky and wanting to forgive her.

She was just about to turn onto Nightingale Lane when she stopped. She dropped her chin onto her chest and just stood there thinking. With a deep sigh, she slowly turned and began the walk back to Magic Row. She headed toward Shiver. She ran as fast as she could.

She burst into the store. There were a few customers scattered about, but Honey didn't care. She marched toward Shiver. "You knew all along. Why didn't you just tell me?"

"It had to come from her," Shiver said.

"Well, I hate her now," Honey said. "She lied

to me."

Shiver's eyebrows rose. She returned a credit card to a customer. "Thank you."

The customer nodded and then glared at Honey. But Honey still didn't care.

"Seems to me there's been a lot of lying going on. One lie doesn't cancel out the others. May I see the locket?"

Honey placed the locket in Shiver's palm. Shiver touched it lightly and then held it so it hung from the silver chain and twirled and sparkled in the light. "This is a special piece." She opened it. "I remember, now, something Astronomer Moon said. 'In most cases, we accept excuses too easily; in our friends, we don't accept excuses easily enough.'"

Shiver set the locket into Honey's palm and closed her fingers around it. "You need to forgive her. But perhaps you need to take care of business with your mother first."

Honey put the necklace into her turtle backpack.

"The locket will be safe with Turtle," Shiver said.

She sat at one of the bistro tables. A wave of guilt and sadness washed over her. The customers left, and Shiver joined Honey.

"How can I ever forgive her? Maybe Kligore is right. Maybe lying is best. Keeping secrets is best. No one gets hurt."

"Really?" Shiver said. "No one gets hurt? What about your mom? What happens when she wants to wear that gorgeous locket tonight and finds it missing? I think that will hurt."

"The party," Honey said. "Harry and I are babysitting."

"Then you better head home. She's probably getting ready right now."

"Maybe I can get it back into her jewelry

167

box without her noticing," Honey said.

"Oh, Honey," Shiver said. "That's not the answer I wanted to hear."

Shiver reached over and a few droplets of her Shivercicle dripped onto the soil of the potted violet. As tiny pink flowers bloomed, she said, "But, I have faith in you Honey Moon. You'll make this right."

168

Honey ran all the way home with all her might and strength. It seemed with every step the silver locket grew heavier and heavier. She couldn't wait to get it back into the jewelry box. She'd finally be in the clear.

She ran hard and fast. She ran up the path to her front door, burst through, and ran straight up the steps. She was now just inches away from unburdening herself—or so she thought.

Honey had stopped just outside her parent's

bedroom when she heard her mother say, "I don't understand. I always keep it in my jewelry box." The door was open. She peeked inside. Her mother and father were all dressed up in their best clothes. Mary Moon was sitting at her vanity looking through the jewelry box.

Honey swallowed. She reached into her backpack, and the locket felt warm. *Probably from all that running,* Honey thought.

"Are you sure you didn't put it someplace else?" Honey heard her dad ask. "Did you take it to the jeweler to be cleaned and forget it?"

"No, no. Mr. Jinx would have called me. It must be here somewhere."

Honey crept closer to her parent's door.

"I'm heartsick," Mary Moon said. "I love that locket, and I really wanted to wear it tonight. Where could it be?"

John moved closer to Mary and put his hand on her shoulder. "I'm certain it will turn up. We'll enlist a full-scale search tomorrow. But, for now, we have to get to going."

Honey could see her mother's face in the vanity mirror. She couldn't remember a time when she had looked so sad and pretty at the same time. When her mother looked up into the mirror, she spotted Honey standing in the doorway. "Oh there you are, Honey," she said.

170

"I was beginning to think you forgot. Harvest already had his sup—"

"I took it. I took your necklace." The words shot out of Honey's mouth like tennis balls from an automatic server gone haywire. "I'm sorry. But it was me. I took it. I didn't mean for it to get lost. I only wanted to try it on and then—"

"Whoa, hold on," her father said. "Come in here."

171

"You took it?" her mother said. "But, Honey, you know that's against the rules. You know how precious that locket is to the family."

Honey lowered her head. She couldn't even look her mother in the eyes. "I know. I know. I just meant to try it on and then return it."

"But how could you have lost it?" John Moon asked.

Honey sighed, and then she told them the whole story. She pulled the necklace out of her backpack and gave it to her mother. "Becky's the one who took it, but it's still my fault. I should never have taken it in the first place." A small shiver ran down Honey's spine. Honey burst into tears, and she threw her arms around her mother's neck. "I'm sorry, Mom. Please forgive me. I'll never touch it again. Ever."

"Of course, I forgive you."

"But there will be consequences," John Moon said. "We'll figure that out in the morning. Right now, your mother and I have a party to attend."

"Yes," Mary Moon said. "Are you certain Becky took it?"

Honey nodded. "Yes. She told me herself just a little while ago. In the park. I'm so mad at her."

"At her?" Mary Moon said. "But you share the guilt."

"I know, but she stole it. I only borrowed it."

Mary Moon shook her head. "Honey. Don't you see? There is no difference."

Honey watched as her father slipped the necklace around her mother's neck and clasped it in the back.

"This is very special to me," Mary Moon said, looking down and fingering the locket. "I'm glad it found its way home."

The silver locket shone brighter than ever.

Honey backed away from her parents, wishing she had never taken the locket but glad they had forgiven her. It didn't make it okay. She had still done something wrong. She would face the consequences, but knowing her parents loved her enough to forgive her was like having a warm blanket wrapped around her shoulders after walking through a cold, hard rain.

"Honey," her mother called. "You know you have to forgive Becky."

"I-I can't," Honey said.

Honey saw disappointment in her mother's eyes as they closed their bedroom door to finish dressing for the party.

∞

"What about consequences for Becky?" she said as she joined Harry and Harvest on the couch. "She still stole it from me, and she's getting away with it."

"Seriously? Really?" Harry said. "You confess to mom that you took her locket and then lied about it, and you're still blaming Becky."

"Yes," Honey said. "All she had to do was give it back to me."

"I bet that was hard for her to do," Harry said. He wiggled Harvest's Headless Horseman Plush Doll at him. Harvest giggled.

"You don't understand," Honey said. "She's my best friend. Was my best friend. How could she steal from me?"

Harry chuckled. "She's still your best friend. You just need to forgive her the same way mom forgave you. Then get back to being friends."

"You just don't get it, Harrold. My best friend stole from me. And lied to me." Honey jumped off the couch. "I'll be upstairs if you need me."

She started up just as her parents started down. She waited for them.

"So, just how beautiful are we?" John Moon asked jokingly.

"Mom looks gorgeous," Harry said. "But sorry, you look like a penguin, Dad."

"Very funny, Harry," John said. "We'll be home around eleven. No shenanigans."

"Don't worry, Dad," Harry said. "I got it under control."

John looked at Honey. "And don't forget. We have some discussing to do tomorrow."

"I know," Honey said.

After her parents were gone, Honey started up the steps again. She got all the way to her room when she heard Harvest cry.

"Now what?" Honey said. She headed back down the steps and saw Harvest sobbing on the couch.

"What's wrong?" Honey asked.

"I'm not sure. But he is crying about that toy. It was right here like ten seconds ago."

"The horseman?" Honey asked.

"Horsey," Harvest cried.

Honey looked around. "I don't know why he loves that thing so much. It's creepy."

"It's Sleepy Hollow," Harry said. "Help me look."

Honey looked around. She searched under the sofa and chairs. She even checked in the kitchen. The toy was gone.

"Funny how things go missing around here," Harry said. "First the locket and now Harvest's toy." Then he laughed. "Ha, maybe Becky took it."

Honey was shocked. She couldn't believe her brother would say something so mean.

177

"Hey, Harry," Honey said. "That's not nice. Don't talk about Becky like that."

Harry flopped into the big armchair near the fireplace. "Why? You were angry at her a few minutes ago."

Honey sat on the couch with Harvest in her lap. "Yeah, but–but she's still my friend."

"Exactly," Harry said. "She's still your friend."

Honey sat for a moment and thought about Becky and her mother and Shiver and the locket.

She felt a glimmer that stretched into a shiver that settled into her shoes. "Thank you, Harry Moon. I understand. Thanks for using some of your brother magic to make me see it."

Harvest clapped. "Shivercicle."

"That's right," Honey said. "Shiver was telling me the same thing."

Harry stood. "Where can that horse be?"

"Horsey," Harvest said.

"I have to forgive her. The same way Mom and Dad forgave me."

"That's how it works," Harry said.

Honey stood up with Harvest in her arms. "It's okay, bro," she said. "I'll find your toy." Then Honey felt it or thought it or noticed it. Another glimmer. She nodded toward the couch. "Look," she said. "It's right there behind the pillow. I see it sticking out."

"No way," Harry said. "We just looked there. And you were just sitting there. I looked under all the cushions too. How'd you do that?"

Honey helped Harvest back to the couch. He grabbed his toy. "Shivercicle."

Harry laughed. "No, Harvest. That's not a Shivercicle."

"But really," Harry said. "Did you do that?"

179

"I–I don't know. Maybe. Let's just say I had a feeling that it was right under our nose. I guess the things we care about most are never very far away."

"Like best friends," Harry said.

"Yeah, like best friends or favorite toys," Honey said. "Look, I'll be right back."

Harry clicked on the TV. "Take your time."

Honey went to her room and called Becky.

"I forgive you," Honey said. "And I'm sorry I got so angry. I'm sorry I said what I said."

"I'm glad," Becky said. "I know I shouldn't have taken it."

"Well, Mom is wearing it to the party tonight. I'm probably grounded until I'm thirty, but you know what? I feel pretty good."

CONSEQUENCES

Saturday morning arrived with buckets of rain pouring on Sleepy Hollow. Honey awoke to the sound of the wind whistling through the trees. But she also awoke to the sound of a clear conscience. It felt good to know that the locket situation was over and things could get back to normal. It also felt great that she had forgiven Becky, and they could be best friends again.

Of course, she still had to talk to her parents and face the consequences.

She found them in the den.

"Good morning," she said, walking into the room. "How was the party?"

"It was very nice," Mary Moon said. "We had a wonderful time."

182

Honey sat in the big, overstuffed armchair. The chair always made her feel secure. It was here that she used to sit with her father or mother while they read stories.

"I really am sorry, Mom. I know how special that locket is."

"It certainly is," John Moon said. "It's priceless, at least to our family."

Honey nodded.

"But, Honey," Mary Moon said, "even though we forgave you, we think some kind of discipline is in order, so you are grounded for a week."

"That's not so bad," Honey said. "Harry said you'd ground me until I was thirty."

Mary laughed. "No, not that long. A week with no phones, no friends."

"I know the drill," Honey said.

"But that's not all," John Moon said.

183

Honey swallowed. Hard. *This can't be good.* "There's more?"

"While we were at the party last night, we saw a notice on the bulletin board," John Moon said. "That new shop, Shiver, is sponsoring a town cleanup next Saturday. Consider yourself a volunteer."

"Ugh, I have to clean up other people's trash?" Honey said.

Her father nodded.

Honey knew it was best not to argue when her father was handing down a sentence. "I guess some hard labor is in order."

"Well, she's giving out free Shivercicles to all the volunteers," her mother said.

"That's nice," Honey said.

"I guess that's all," John Moon said. "You can be excused.

184

Honey didn't move right away.

"Is there something else?" her mother asked.

"I–I just wanted to tell you that I called Becky last night and told her I forgive her."

Mary Moon clapped her hands. "That's terrific, Honey."

"I'm proud of you," John Moon said.

Honey stood up and walked toward the den door. Then she stopped and turned around,

"But, Mom, there's still a problem."

"What's that?" Mary asked.

"Consequences. Doesn't Becky get consequences?"

Mary and John exchanged glances. "Well, dear," Mary said. "That's not for you to decide. Yours was to simply forgive."

Honey trudged back to her room. A week's grounding wasn't too bad. Although, life without a cell phone was pretty awful. She'd have to get all the news and do all her talking at school. And here it was Saturday with nothing to do. She looked around her room. "I suppose I could do some cleanup."

After getting dressed in jeans and a blue tee, Honey heard the house phone ring and then her mother calling, "Honey, phone." She looked at Turtle and felt a slight shiver wiggle down her back.

Honey raced to the kitchen. "But I'm

grounded."

"I'm making an exception. Three minutes."

Honey picked up the phone.

"Hello?"

It was Becky.

"I'm grounded. For a week," Becky said. "Your mom called my mom, and now I'm grounded, and I have to volunteer at the cleanup next week."

Honey smiled wider than she had smiled in a quite a few days. "I'm so glad."

"What?" Becky asked.

"No, not that you got grounded, not exactly. I'm just glad we'll be volunteering together."

After a long, hard, silent week Honey finally

made it to the next Saturday. She was thrilled that she would get to see Shiver. Being grounded meant she couldn't visit the shop after school.

She dressed quickly that morning in old jeans and a flannel shirt. Cleaning up was messy business, and the tourists who came through Sleepy Hollow had a tendency to be quite messy. There was no doubt there would be tons of trash—candy wrappers, paper cups, and probably orange, sticky goo to clean from the park benches. The Pumpkin Puke gum was pretty popular, and kids liked to stick it under the benches.

As she made her way to the park, which was being used as the staging area for the massive workday, Honey hoped Shiver would be there. She also hoped there would be plenty of rubber gloves.

When Honey saw Shiver, she ran toward her. Shiver beamed the same welcoming smile she always wore, but this time she had her purple hair piled high on her head. Shiver was standing behind an old-fashioned-looking cart on wheels.

It was painted purple with lots of tiny Shivercicles painted all over it, and of course, the name SHIVER was painted in bright yellow.

Honey threw her arms around her." Oh, Shiver," she said. "I've missed you."

"And I've missed you, Honey. I take it your absence this week meant things got worked out."

"Yes," Honey said. "I'm grounded."

"Small price to pay. But the truth looks good on you."

"It feels good," Honey said. "But I also have to volunteer today."

"Your name is already on my list," Shiver said. "I assigned you and Becky Young to the lake area. Just meet back here in a couple of hours."

"Gotcha," Honey said.

"I'm glad you and Becky worked it out also. Forgiveness is a beautiful thing."

"Me too," Honey said. She pulled on her rubber gloves, grabbed a couple of plastic trash bags, and ran off toward the lake. Who would have thought it could feel so good to spend a Saturday cleaning gum off park benches?

Becky was already hard at work. Her first bag was nearly full.

"Look," Becky said. "My bag is already half full of trash. People are gross."

"Yeah," Honey said. "Half full. It's just like you to see it half full and not half empty."

Becky laughed. "I'm glad we're friends again."

"Yeah, but I was thinking that I haven't really spoken to Isabel or Claire since this whole thing went down. Even at school. It was like we were all normal again."

"We are normal," Becky said. She shoved a

paper cup into her bag.

Honey reached under a bush and yanked out a plastic bag. "Yuck. I know we're normal," Honey said. "But I never apologized to them."

"Oh," Becky said. "You actually thought Claire would take a necklace?"

Honey laughed. "No, not really. I didn't really know what to think."

190

The two hours went by quicker than Honey thought they would. She and Becky were among the first back to Shiver. And among the first to get Shivercicles. Honey got blueberry. Becky got pomegranate, which made Honey's eyes roll. "Pomegranate? Really?"

"It's very healthy," Shiver said. "Antioxidants."

Honey and Becky were sitting on one of the newly cleaned benches to eat their Shivercicles when the Phantom Lustro pulled up to the curb. It was so shiny black Honey could see her and Becky reflected in the doors.

"Uh oh," Honey said. "Here comes Mayor Kligore."

"To help? Mayor Kligore pick up trash? Maybe a normal mayor would but not him."

"I don't think he's here to pick up trash," Honey said. "Come on. Let's check it out."

They ran toward Shiver as Kligore marched across the park. He walked with balled up fists straight toward Shiver.

"Gonna be a showdown," Honey said.

"Right here in Sleepy Hollow," Becky said.

"Mayor Kligore," Shiver said, "how nice of you to volunteer."

Honey laughed when she heard that.

"I did not come here to volunteer," the mayor sneered. "I came to tell you that although I am still haunted by that infernal dream, I will prevail in my war against you and Samson Dupree and the infernal Harry Moon."

"Dream?" Becky asked.

"Yeah, he dreams about being chased by an army of Shivercicles. He's, like, really upset about it."

Becky laughed. "Shivercicles can't hurt you."

Honey shrugged. "It's not the Shivercicles he's afraid of. It's what they mean."

Becky wrinkled her brow.

"Listen," Honey said. "It's about to get good."

Honey and Becky moved a little closer to Shiver.

"Oh, dear," Shiver said. "I truly am sorry about the dream thingy."

"No, you aren't," Kligore said.

"Of course, I am," Shiver said. "I feel very sorry for you."

"Well, you shouldn't feel sorry for me. I am the best mayor—ever!" Mayor Kligore said. "And besides, I figured it out. Those Shivercicles are a sign. A sign to me that I can't get rid of you. You're like a wad of Pumpkin Puke gum stuck to my shoe. I must let you stay in Sleepy Hollow just as I let that despicable Samson Dupree stay. I don't know how you do it but–but whatever power you and he have is not easily shaken."

"Now you're getting it," Shiver said.

"But know this," Mayor Kligore continued, "I will be keeping my eye on you."

"You better," Honey said.

Kligore turned toward Honey.

Honey gasped. The mayor's beady little eyes seemed to glow red.

"And you! I will keep my eye on you. Seems I have two Moons to worry about."

"Yes, you do," Honey said. "And by the way, Mayor, I didn't take your advice. I told the truth."

Kligore's face went pale. "I know. I know everything."

Shiver fake coughed.

"Almost everything," the mayor said.

"The truth will set you free," Honey said. "Well, tomorrow, I'll be set free."

A big shiver wriggled down Honey's back.

"Are you all right?" Shiver asked.

"Just a shiver," Honey asked.

Shiver laughed. "Well, everybody needs a shiver once in a while."

"Stop talking like that!" Mayor Kligore said. "Now I must be getting back to Folly Farm to plan my next . . . publicity campaign for Sleepy Hollow."

"Ahh, so that's what you're calling your evil acts," Shiver said.

Kligore looked around. A small crowd was gathering. "Shhhh, never mind." He stormed off toward the Phantom Lustro where Cherry stood with the back door opened.

"Mind if I come by the store after my grounding is up?" Honey asked.

"I'll be expecting you, Honey Moon. I always was."

Honey smiled. "So will the mayor stop having that dream now?"

"Maybe," Shiver said. "But I think his real nightmare has just begun."

It was getting late. The sun had already set, and the sky was dark. Honey had had a big day. She volunteered for the clean-up, confronted Mayor Kligore, and totally made up with Becky. But Honey still had one more thing to do. She and Becky were friends again and probably would be forever. But there was Claire and Isabela to consider. She had falsely suspected them of stealing the locket. She knew Claire was feeling hurt, and Isabela thought she was all alone again in Sleepy Hollow. She might have had all week, practically, to talk to them, but for some reason, asking forgiveness two more times was daunting. Until now.

Honey set out to make matters right. She stopped first at Claire's house and asked forgiveness, and Claire, being Claire, shrugged and then socked her in the shoulder. That was just fine with Honey. "Thanks, Honey," Claire said. "It was pretty mean of you to think I'd take that necklace. I don't even like jewelry— unless it's a Super Bowl ring."

Isabela was so glad to see Honey she threw her arms around her and said, "I'm so glad we can still be friends, but I understand. Losing something so precious is a tragedy—I know that for sure—and I really don't want to lose you."

197

As Honey was heading home, the sun was dropping in the sky, and the town was closing up for the night. She thought it could be fun to stop at Shiver just to say hello and to explain that she had made up with everyone and they were best friends again. She strolled down Magic Row and was just about to cross the street when she saw Shiver walk out onto the all-weather blue carpet that ran from the door to the curb. She stopped for a moment, and Honey was pretty sure Shiver saw her, but she didn't wave or call Honey over. Instead, she seemed to give Honey a tiny, little wink. At least, Honey was pretty sure it was a wink—

hard to know for certain from across the street. She liked to think it was wink.

Shiver turned away from the curb back toward the store, and as she walked, the blue carpet rolled up behind her. When Shiver opened the door to the shop, she glanced back over her shoulder one last time, her eyes lit with fireworks, and stepped inside. The front door to the Shivercicle store shrunk until it disappeared. The shutters around the windows slapped shut across the glass with a bang, and the roof started to collapse with a clatter. Then, in a blink, the entire store went POOF. In its place was simply nothing—as if the store had never existed in the first place. Shiver and the establishment had disappeared, rolled up and vanished. Honey stood and watched in amazement with her heart beating out of her chest and eyes as wide as saucers. A deep sadness swept over her. "She's gone?"

Honey rubbed her eyes. "It can't be." She opened her eyes again and saw Shiver standing on the pavement where the store had just been. Honey gasped and shouted, "SHIVER!"

Consequences

She ran across the street, but by the time she got there, Shiver was gone again. A silver locket dangled in mid-air. It was the most beautiful locket Honey had ever seen. Honey reached for the necklace, and a note dropped from it.

It read:

Dear Honey, wear this always, remember to feel for the glimmer, and whenever you need me just give a little shiver.

P.S. Bring your friends by for Shivercicles when the Shoppe opens at 11 a.m. tomorrow.

199

K ids ask us all the time, "Where do you get your ideas for all the Harry and Honey Moon stories?"

Well, ideas are everywhere. You can find them watching the news, inside a fortune cookie, talking with a friend, or even walking down the street in the small, artsy community of Covington, Kentucky. And that is exactly where we came across the idea for the book *Shiver*.

Shiver is a real store in a real town run by an incredible woman named Lynn Dziad. She opened Shiver in June of 2017 after selling her amazing and sometimes strange, sometimes healthy homemade popsicles at music festivals for years. Everyone loved her Shivercicles.

Lynn said she still gets her own shivers when someone bites into one of the pops and says, "Wow! This is great!" Who knew that freezing chocolate chip cookies inside a coating of white chocolate, dipping the whole thing in blue, and calling it Cookie Monster would work? But it did. People stood in line to gobble up her wonderful Shivercicles.

The idea for an actual frozen-magic flavor shop had been in Lynn's mind for a long, long time. It just took a teaspoon of courage to step away from her "normal" job and take the plunge into running the business full time. Lynn said, "Opening up the shop was like walking off a cliff and building an airplane on the way down." She said she made lots of mistakes and struggled a little at first, but it was important to learn from her mistakes and try again. And again sometimes.

It was while Lynn and a friend were hanging out that she settled on the name Shiver for her store. They were just tossing names around, one after the other, until finally she hit upon Shiver and it stuck. Her tagline, "You don't have to be bad to feel good," came about the same way. Ideas are like that. Just keep tossing things around until just the right notion or word feels right. "You'll know it when you hear it," Lynn said.

Like Honey Moon, Lynn needed good friends who helped her muster up the courage to strike out on her own. It seemed Lynn was always the friend who brought homemade ice cream—also with strange flavor combinations—and homemade pops to parties and holiday celebrations. Everyone encouraged her to start a business. So, one day, she said, "I've got this idea. Why not try it now?" Today, SHIVER is a brick-and-mortar business that draws block-long lines of happy customers anxious to choose their favorite flavor. Maybe it's a Bananas Foster or a Plum Tarragon Shivercicle.

Lynn advises Honey Moon readers to "Find out what you enjoy. You have to like what you do." For this frozen-flavor magician, everything she tastes makes her wonder, "Can I turn this into a Shivercicle?"

Lynn loves owning her own business. Every success is celebrated, and every mistake just makes her stronger, more determined, and courageous. "When I make a mistake, I step back, regroup, and focus. And then I try again. It's all about being brave just as Honey Moon is always saying."

203

But why ice pops? "I like the old-timey feel of them. You can run with them. You can take them on a walk to the park. Try running with a huge banana split!"

Some of the Harry Moon creative team happened upon Shiver on a visit to Covington, Kentucky and were wowed by the lines of people outside her door waiting to buy a Shivercicle. They walked inside and fell in love with the store and the whole brilliant idea of magic on a stick. It just had to become part of Sleepy Hollow.

"I love Harry and Honey Moon," said Lynn. "I am creating some very special Sleepy Hollow Shivercicles for our readers!"

And now, Shiver is forever frozen in our stories just a couple of doors down from the Sleepy Hollow Magic Shoppe. It is a welcome and magical addition to an already magical town.

204

If you would like to say hi to the real Shiver or order a Shiver T-shirt, go to her Facebook page, facebook.com/Shivercicles. We think Lynn Dziad is a very cool and special lady.

Dear Reader,

Wow! Honey really got herself into a pickle this time. She almost fell for Mayor Kligore's tricks and kept right on telling lies. That would have been a disaster. I'm so glad Honey decided to tell her mom the truth about the locket. The truth is always the best policy even if there are consequences, like getting grounded.

It's not always easy to stand up for yourself or confront a bully or tell the truth. But remember this: being brave is about doing the right thing even when you feel scared or anxious. It's okay to be scared. It's okay to cry. When Honey discovered her friend Becky took the necklace, she felt angry, and that's okay too. What you do with the anger is important.

Honey thought about it and was able to forgive Becky. Forgiveness doesn't mean it's okay; it doesn't mean forgetting. Forgiveness means you're going to stop feeling angry. Always feeling anger toward some-one is the pits.

Honey loves Becky and would never want to lose her as a friend. Honey faced her fears, told the truth, learned to forgive, and took the consequences of her actions with good cheer.

In this story, Honey also discovered something else about herself when she met Shiver. I'm so glad Honey met Shiver because now Honey has a good adult friend, a mentor, someone to help her be brave and strong and stand up for herself like she did in this story.

Shiver helped Honey see that she has a special magic that she can use to make people feel better or even restore something lost or broken. It's a pretty powerful kind of magic, but you know what? If you think about it, you have that magic also.

I bet you have lots of chances to help someone find something they've lost, maybe even their good mood. I bet you can help someone feel better about herself maybe by offering forgiveness or writing a letter or maybe even choosing to hang out with someone who needs a friend. It's all about putting others first, and that, my friends, is a very powerful and heroic thing to do.

Love,

Joyce

MARK ANDREW POE

Honey Moon creator Mark Andrew Poe never thought about creating a town where kids battled right and wrong. His dream was to love and care for animals, specifically his friends in the rabbit community.

Along the way, Mark became successful in all sorts of interesting careers. He entered the print and publishing world as a young man, and his company did really, really well. Mark also became a popular and nationally sought-after health care advocate for the care and well-being of rabbits.

Years ago, Mark came up with the idea of a story about a young boy with a special connection to a world of magic, all revealed through a remarkable rabbit friend.

Mark worked on his idea for several years before building a collaborative creative team to help him bring his idea to life.

Harry Moon was born. The team was thrilled when Mark introduced Harry's enchanting sister, Honey Moon. Boy, did she pack an unexpected punch!

In 2014, Mark began a multi-book project to launch Harry Moon and Honey Moon into the youth marketplace. Harry and Honey are kids who understand the difference between right and wrong. Kids who tangle with magic and forces unseen in a town where "every day is Halloween night." Today, Mark and the creative team continue to work on the many stories of Harry and Honey and the characters of Sleepy Hollow. He lives in suburban Chicago with his wife and his twenty-five rabbits.

Honey Moon's
DNA

Builds friendships that matter
Goes where she is needed
Helps fellow classmates
Speaks her mind
Honors her body
Does not categorize others
Loves to have a blast
Seeks wisdom from adults
Desires to be brave
Sparkles away
And, of course, loves her mom

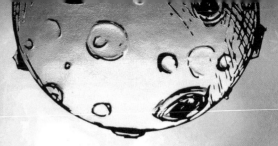

Coming Soon!
More Magical Adventures

POSTER INSIDE!

HONEY MOON
SHADES AND SHENANIGANS

SOFI BENITEZ